"Beware of what you start with me, Sara

"You may discover you've bitten off more than you can chew."

"I don't know what you're talking about." She tried to push him away, but his hard, muscled body was pressed against hers making the effort useless. "Turn me loose," she said with as much bravado as she could muster.

"The word is *please*."

Sara remained silent.

Brody cupped the back of her neck with his hand. She tried pushing against it. But his hand was like a vise. Slowly, deliberately, he forced her head forward until their lips were barely touching.

"Please," he insisted.

Everything seemed to come to a standstill at the taste of his warm breath and his lips brushing against hers. But somehow Sara managed to remain firm. "I'll not say please to a man who thinks he can get away with rudeness!"

Praise for DeLoras Scott's previous work

The Lady and the Outlaw
"A tremendous tale that keeps the reader laughing...
You'll long remember this book."
—*Rendezvous*

The Devil's Kiss
"...a great satirical Western romance...
the story line is humorous,
and the lead characters both first rate."
—*Affaire de Coeur*

Bittersweet
"...Ms. Scott makes an impressive debut
and ensures herself a spot on readers' bookshelves."
—*Romantic Times Magazine*

SARA
AND THE
ROGUE

DELORAS SCOTT

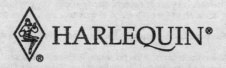

HARLEQUIN®

TORONTO • NEW YORK • LONDON
AMSTERDAM • PARIS • SYDNEY • HAMBURG
STOCKHOLM • ATHENS • TOKYO • MILAN • MADRID
PRAGUE • WARSAW • BUDAPEST • AUCKLAND

ISBN 0-373-29190-6

SARA AND THE ROGUE

This edition published by arrangement with Harlequin Books S.A.

® and TM are trademarks of the publisher. Trademarks indicated with
® are registered in the United States Patent and Trademark Office, the
Canadian Trade Marks Office and in other countries.

Visit us at www.eHarlequin.com

Printed in U.S.A.

Please address questions and book requests to:
Harlequin Reader Service
U.S.: 3010 Walden Ave., P.O. Box 1325, Buffalo, NY 14269
Canadian: P.O. Box 609, Fort Erie, Ont. L2A 5X3

To my beloved. May he rest in peace.

Prologue

Territory of Kansas

Sara Miles leaned low in the saddle and nervously reigned her galloping horse into the narrow gorge that trailed between a long series of red rock monoliths. Ahead, the men had the horses and mules running at breakneck speed, their hooves pounding the deep alkali dust and churning it into gritty, blinding clouds.

Sara pulled her bandanna over her nose and batted her eyelids, trying to keep them clear. Poor Joe, who brought up the rear, had to be getting the worst of it.

Had the "mighty" Brody Hawkins and his Indian friend managed to lead her and her three men into the gorge before the Pawnee or Comanche warriors had caught sight of them?

A sudden, high-pitched yipping echoed around the passage walls, curdling Sara's blood. She knew instinctively that her prayers had not been answered. Fear crawled up her spine with the legs of a tarantula and her gloved hands had broken out in sweat. They hadn't escaped undetected. The Indians were following.

Her blond hair flying as wild as a banshee's, Sara whipped the ends of the reins across her horse's rump, desperate for more speed. The ten mules she led were slowing them down. But her entire future depended on those mules and she'd be dammed if she'd let a band of Indians take them.

Seemingly out of nowhere, Brody Hawkins pulled up alongside her, adjusting his horse's speed to hers. She didn't have to worry about the Indians killing her; Brody seemed intent on taking care of that. The path appeared to be too narrow to accommodate two horses side by side, running as fast as their legs would carry them. Surely she and Brody were going to be cut to pieces by the jagged walls.

Brody motioned for her to release the mules.

Sara's throat tightened. She shook her head and tried to get in front of him, but he kept his horse right alongside hers. His face set in stone, he moved his gelding dangerously close, leaving Sara no room to avoid him. He looped his reins around his saddle horn.

"No-o-o," Sara yelled as she watched him draw a knife from his boot. She tried to slap him with the reins, but with one quick slice, he'd cut the lead rope she held in her hand. Freed, her mules slowed down. Brody might as well have sank the blade into her heart.

Brody also dropped back, meaning he intended to have Joe release his animals. Sara wanted to wretch. The unconscionable villain was making sure she didn't win their bet!

"He didn't knock me from the saddle because he's getting his way," she muttered bitterly.

Dirt continued to fly in her face, but Sara was too furious to care. She made a silent vow that when this was all over, she'd shoot Brody in the knee...both knees. Maybe she'd end up losing everything, but for the rest of his life he'd remember what he'd done.

Sara rode into the open, the bright, afternoon sunlight bringing tears to her eyes. The moment she saw two of her men, her heart leaped with joy. All wasn't lost. They had a tight grip on their lead ropes and were busily trying to calm their mules. Half of the original forty had been saved.

"Buck! Mack!" Sara yelled as she dismounted. "No matter what Brody Hawkins says, you are not to turn those mules loose!"

Brody rode up behind her, leaping from his horse as it came to a sliding halt. Her third man, Joe, followed, and as she had suspected, he no longer had his string of mules.

"Sara, there's a cave up there," Brody said, his words snapping in the hot air like a quick staccato. He pointed to the spot, his towering figure blocking the sun. "I want you in it. Take Mack's mount."

Sara marched up to him and planted her heels in the ground. That the top of her head barely reached his shoulder was of little significance. "I'll not take orders from you and I'll not move until you assure me the rest of my mules will be safe."

"You men dismount," Brody called to Buck and Mack, completely ignoring her ultimatum. "We're going to send the rest of the mules back down the passage."

"You'll do no such thing!" Sara fumed. Her men were actually following his orders!

"It'll give us time to position ourselves on either side behind the boulders," he explained to the men. "Grab your rifles. Mack, take the one from Sara's saddle. We can pick off the renegades as they come into the open."

Sara stomped a heel down on Brody's foot. "Oh, no. In the first place, if I go anywhere it will be on Buckets's back. I'm not about to leave my horse to those renegades! They already have twenty of my mules. Secondly, you have no right to order me or my—"

Brody grabbed Sara around the waist and in one quick swoop, planted her atop Mack's mount. "Get in that cave."

"No!" She slid out of the saddle only to be hoisted back up.

"You pick the damndest times for a squabble! There are twenty some odd savages at our backs...."

Sara squared her shoulders. "I want my horse and mules!" she demanded.

"I'll give you this warning once, lady. If you don't get in that cave and let me handle this, I'll shoot your confounded mules right now, one at a time."

He walked to where his horse stood, grabbed his rifle and took aim at the closest mule.

"You wouldn't!" Sara said confidently.

Brody's finger tightened on the trigger.

"Stop!" she yelled. How much more was she going to have to sacrifice? "I'll go to the cave, but on my own horse. Brody, I can't let them take her from me."

"Sara," he said in a gentler voice, "the Indians had to have spotted the paint. I don't think they know how many of us there are, but if the mare is missing they'll know something's not right."

As he turned away, Sara picked up the reins and nudged Mack's horse forward with her heels. He'd left her with no recourse but to do as she had been told. Tears stung her eyes. She would never see her beautiful horse, Buckets, again.

"Mack, take the horses and secure them behind the big boulders." For a brief moment, Brody watched Sara head the buckskin up the rocky incline. "And no matter what happens," he called to her, "stay hidden!"

When Sara reached the cave, it took several hard

kicks to get the buckskin to go inside. She didn't blame him; the stench of animal excrement was overwhelming. Hopefully the previous owner had left and didn't plan on returning soon.

Sara quickly slid from the saddle. The deep cave offered plenty of room to hide. After tying the reins to a rock, she returned to the entrance and peeked out. A green bush hid part of the opening and allowed a perfect spot for viewing.

Sara was just in time to see the mules being chased back through the gorge. A heavy groan passed her dried, cracked lips. Though she understood what Brody was doing, it did nothing to alleviate her disappointment.

Below, the four men had taken strategic positions and, rifles raised, waited. Where had Brody's Indian friend gone? she wondered. Maybe to get help. Maybe he just ran away.

Sara shrugged her shoulders in an attempt to rid the tightness. There was no longer any reason to remain so tense. They were all safe now. The Indians wouldn't be taking scalps this day. The men could easily pick off each one as they rode into the clearing. Of course if Brody and the others were really fortunate, the braves would be satisfied with just getting the mules. If. A mighty big word.

After several wiggles, Sara made herself as comfortable as possible on a rock, then waited. She raised her arm and attempted to wipe the sweat from her forehead with her sleeve. A useless motion. Her face was filthy.

Minutes ticked by. Where were the Indians? Sara wondered. They should have already ridden out of the canyon. The silence had become unnerving. Obviously they had turned back.

When a good thirty minutes had passed, Sara couldn't stand it any longer. Brody was being overly cautious. She stood and opened her mouth to call below when she heard a noise. She recognized the drum as the beat grew louder, throbbing at her temples. The Indians were still there. They hadn't been foolish enough to ride into an ambush.

As the hours passed, the incessant beating had Sara pacing the hard-packed earth and holding her ears. Why did they keep pounding that blasted drum? To remind the men of the existing danger? She didn't know about the others, but it was certainly working on her. Her nerves were completely frayed.

A cool breeze brushed Sara's skin, making her shiver. She glanced at the horse. She hadn't unsaddled him in case she needed to leave quickly.

Her mouth feeling as though she'd gargled with sand, she grabbed the canteen from the pommel and took a long drink. Satisfied, she cupped her hand and carefully poured water for the horse to drink.

With the sun quickly fading behind the huge rocks, Sara pulled the extra boxes of shells from the saddlebags and piled them by the cave entrance. After making sure Mack's rifle was loaded, she leaned it against a rock near the shells. The bedroll was placed on the ground, far enough inside to help ward off the chill but close enough to the rifle and shells should she need them.

Sara couldn't shake the feeling that the worst was yet to come. Would she and the others still be alive by tomorrow's end? Would she never see Brody again?

She started to remove her leather chaps then thought better of it. Exhausted, she sat on the bedroll and rested her back against the cave wall, but her calves still ached from the tension.

It was a wonder Brody hadn't offered her to the Indians as a sacrifice, she thought bitterly, even though she knew in her heart she was simply trying to get back at him for making her forfeit the mules.

To Sara's relief, night fell. Everyone would be safe until dawn. Anyone with half a mind knew Indians didn't attack in the dark.

Jolted from a deep sleep, Sara leaped to her feet. How could she have dozed off? What had awakened her?

The drum had stopped.

A man's scream pierced the air.

Sara ran to the cave entrance. Indians couldn't be

attacking. It was still dark. She couldn't see a thing below.

Shots were exchanged.

She'd never trust an Indian in the dark again.

More shots.

Another agonizing scream.

Deadening silence.

Sara's entire body shook. Brody! Had anything happened to him? Was he dead or alive? If only she could run to him and tell him of her true feelings. No, he wouldn't want to hear it.

As Sara strained to see something...anything...a circle of small fires began being lit. She stiffened. Five Indians dragged a naked white man to a stake that had been sunk into the ground, while another danced circles and waved what appeared to be scalps. From her men?

Her gaze shifted back to Brody who was now tied to the stake. She couldn't see his face clearly from this distance, but his size alone identified him. One muscled arm hung in an unnatural way at his side. He was still alive, but how much more torture would he be forced to endure before they killed him? Besides the broken arm, his face and body appeared to be badly bruised.

With tears leaving tracks down her cheeks, Sara snatched up the rifle.

Even though a shot would give her position away,

she'd rather see Brody dead than tortured. A brave stepped up, his knife blade shining in the firelight.

Sara raised her rifle.

She couldn't kill all the savages before they got to her, but she could take Brody out of his misery.

The brave moved, blocking the shot meant to end Brody's life.

Sara gritted her teeth as the bastard slowly, deliberately ran the blade down the center of Brody's broad chest, leaving a trail of blood. Sara sobbed. She'd felt the blade of the knife as if it were cutting her. She had never seen a braver man than Brody. He stared straight into the brave's eyes and never let a sound escape his lips.

Sara curled her finger around the trigger. The Indian had moved and she now had a clear shot. "Forgive me, darling," she whispered.

Damnable tears blurred her vision and she had to remove her hand to brush them away. "Tears aren't going to help now, girl," she muttered.

Stiffening her determination, she looked below. Apparently Brody said something that had infuriated the tall, lean brave. Again he raised the knife, but this time in a stabbing position.

Her hand shaking, Sara returned her finger to the trigger.

This time she aimed the end of the rifle at the Indian. She'd take care of him first, then Brody. But before she could pull a shot off, another brave jumped forward, stopping the raised hand in midair. They appeared to be arguing. Then all disappeared behind the fires, leaving Brody alone, still strapped to the pole.

Sara lost all track of time as she stood staring at the only man she'd ever truly loved. He hadn't moved a muscle and the Indians had remained hidden by the dark. She tried thinking of ways to rescue Brody. Had the Indians left? Should she try to free him? But she didn't have a knife, and if she tried to untie him she'd have to enter the ring of fire.

As if Brody knew what she was thinking, he turned his head and looked directly toward her. He shook his head slowly, just enough for her to get his message. His damp black hair hung in his eyes, but even as bad as he had been mistreated, he continued to stand tall on both feet and hold his head high.

Sara dropped to her knees. "Oh, Brody," she whispered, "I don't know what to do."

Though the short nap earlier had helped, she was still exhausted and her legs were as weak as a newborn colt's. Hopefully an opportunity would present itself tomorrow. The wait had allowed her to think clearly. She and Brody were still alive. As long as Brody lived and she remained free, there was the possibility of escape. Caught, they had no chance at all. Besides, someone below was on his side or he'd already be dead.

Sara squeezed her eyes shut, bringing Brody's face

to mind. "I ought to let you die," she muttered angrily. "You're the one who got us in this mess."

A heavy sigh left her throat. That wasn't exactly true. She'd been warned from the beginning to stay away from him.

He had been the flame and she the moth.

She'd done everything wrong. She should have told him about the attack on his freight wagons instead of trying to prove she could handle anything just as well as he could. Even though she'd been insane with jealousy, she'd only ended up hurting herself. And since she was looking at everything honestly, who had made the wager?

Sara opened her eyes and stared into the dark void. It had all started so innocently. Great hopes, lost dreams. She should never have fallen in love. She should never have moved to Leavenworth.

Chapter One

Fort Leavenworth, Kansas
Eighteen months earlier

Sara Miles sat impatiently in the waiting room, awaiting the fort commander. The private behind the nearby desk had assured her several times that as soon as his meeting was over, Colonel Singleton would see her, but only for a brief moment.

"He's very busy," the private had explained.

Sara shifted positions. Her rear had gone numb after sitting on the confounded wooden bench for so long. The freckle-faced private's words had been a repeat of what others had told her. Hamish Goodman had gone so far as to say Colonel Singleton seldom gave his time to civilians, unless they were high-ranked.

"Gives us common folk to one of his subordinates," Hamish had grumbled.

"He'll see me," Sara had stated.

"A twenty-dollar gold piece says you ain't gonna see the inside of the man's office."

"I'll take that bet." She wasn't about to inform Hamish that she'd also heard the bachelor colonel had an eye for the women.

Now here I wait, Sara thought. She looked over at the private and caught him staring at her with a moonstruck look on his face. Embarrassed, he quickly looked away. Sara hoped she'd get the same reaction from the colonel. She straightened the folds of her gray wool skirt

"Miss Miles?"

Sara turned to see a distinguished man walking toward her. She judged him to be around fortysomething and quite impressive in his tailored uniform.

"I apologize for the delay. I had an officers' meeting to attend."

Sara anointed him with her best smile, accepted his hand and stood. She had already learned something about the gentleman. His uniform, perfectly groomed hair and side-whiskers told her he was a prideful man.

"I'm Colonel Singleton. What can I do for you?"

Sara pressed her shoulders back, just enough to enhance her shapely bosom, but not enough to make the act appear blatant. A hint of a smile told her she definitely had his attention.

"If it's all right with you, Colonel, I'd prefer discussing my business in your office."

"I'm sorry but—"

A slight slide of her hand along her small waist was enough to leave a hint of possible pleasures to come. "I promise not to take but a minute of your time."

"Would you like me to handle this, Colonel?" the private eagerly asked.

"Private Black, no warm-blooded man in his right mind could turn his back on a pair of large brown eyes and hair of gold," Colonel Singleton said gallantly.

Elation filled Sara's very being. She had arrived determined that whatever it took, short of bedding and murder, she would not leave until she had what she'd come for.

"Though we have never met," Sara stated when they were alone, "I'm sure you remember my brother, Edmond, and my father, Harold Miles." She glanced around his sparse office that had a masculine feel.

The Colonel's face, leathered from hours in the sun, brightened. "You can't be Sara, the little girl Harold always talked about? The one he referred to as mouse?"

Sara nodded.

"I shared many a fine time with both. They were good men. I sympathize with your loss."

Sara moved to one of the straight-backed wooden chairs and sat. She had finally made it into the colonel's office. Hamish would have a fit when he found out he owed her a twenty-dollar gold piece. "Thank you, but though the memories still hurt, it has been over a year since the accident and I must continue on with my own life."

"Indeed you must!" The Colonel sat on the edge of his desk and leaned forward, placing her small hand in his. "You must have a reason for coming to see me. How can I be of help, my dear?"

Sara gently pulled her hand from his, then flipped her fan open. "My, it is a bit warm in here," she commented.

The Colonel straightened. "My apologies for being so thoughtless. Would you care for something to drink?"

"Water would be fine."

He walked to a side table. "Harold always said you were the biggest asset to his company." After handing her a filled glass, he went to the window and looked out over the parade grounds.

"And I've proven over the past year that I'm also quite capable of running a freighting company on my own. All the shipments continued being delivered to the forts on time and in good condition." She sipped her water. "I'm here for one reason. It's time for the contracts to be renewed."

The Colonel faced her, his surprise obvious. Just as she had suspected, had he known her purpose he wouldn't have met with her at all.

"I assumed that Miles and Son would be closing

their doors. Am I to understand that you, a woman of such a delicate nature, plan to carry on where your father and brother left off?''

Sara ground her teeth. Must she forever put up with men's opinions of what a woman could or couldn't do? ''I don't see where being a female has anything to do with it. I've managed quite well since the loss of my family.

''But you'll be working with hard men, most of whom aren't a bit trustworthy.''

''I've been around men like that for most of my life, Colonel.''

''Surely your father explained how the men at the forts look forward to shipments of food and other necessities, especially after such a hard winter.''

''May I again remind you that I've been doing that for the past year. Discovering a woman would be handling everything should make no difference. Especially since I've already proven my capabilities.''

''Soon the wagons will be moving again. What if you decide to up and quit because you've fallen in love and want to raise a family? Women do that, you know! Then what happens to the men and families at the forts?''

''I would never let that happen.''

''That's easy to say now. No. Giving contracts to—''

''Colonel—'' she joined him at the window ''—I have moved the company here to Leavenworth and renamed it Miles Freighting. I have spent most of my inheritance purchasing Hamish Goodman's company so I can enlarge my carrying capacity." It wasn't exactly true, but saying so gave a strong backing to her cause.

Sara bit her lip. She had to keep control of her temper. So much depended on this man's decision and he was about to reject her simply because she was a woman!

Singleton was at a loss for words. She was right. She had proven she was capable, and by all rights she should get the contracts. Still...

He opened his mouth to say something when Sara abruptly headed for the door. Before he could speak, she suddenly spun around and faced him, her large chocolate-brown eyes sparkling.

"You're being a fool," Sara said softly. "Your arguments have no validity. I have even made arrangements to get the supplies to the forts a week ahead of schedule." Seeing she had recaptured his attention, she returned to the chair she'd just vacated and pressed on. "Think of it. Ham, bacon, sacks of coffee, sugar, potatoes, dried apples and peaches, flour, meal, beans...whatever...will have less time to spoil."

The Colonel crossed his arms over his chest. "And how would you do that?"

"I'm going to use mules instead of oxen."

He cocked a bushy brow. "Mules? Oxen can eat their way to market. Furthermore, they become a source of food if the bullwhackers need it. Mules need fodder.''

"I'll carry fodder in the wagons."

"You'll reduce your cargo capacity."

"Remember? I just bought Goodman's company. Being able to supply enough cargo space isn't a matter of contention. I want these contracts, Colonel, and I deserve them."

The Colonel released a heavy sigh. "I can't argue with a single thing you've said. Very well. The contracts are yours. But I'm adding a condition."

"A condition?"

"Yes. If you're late with even one shipment, I cancel the contract. Is that agreed?"

Sara nodded. "Agreed."

"The papers will be ready for your signature in two days."

Miles Freighting had just negotiated its first contract. If she were a man, she'd get drunk!

"You're a very convincing lady." Colonel Singleton walked her toward the door. "I feel sorry for the men you'll be dealing with in the future." Humor clearly threaded his words.

"Why?"

"They have no idea what is in store for them. You, my dear, have the face of an angel and the guts and determination of a man." He suddenly burst out laughing. "What a combination."

He reached for the doorknob. "A party is being

given tonight for a senator who's visiting the fort. He's very influential and extremely interested in military affairs. I'd consider it an honor if you'd accompany me to the occasion.''

"I would be delighted.''

"Perhaps he can supply you with financiers eager to tap into the riches brought on by so many families moving west.''

"Perhaps he can.''

Chapter Two

Hamish Goodman scurried along the walk, his shoulders hunched forward. The fog blanketing Leavenworth thickened as he approached the Missouri River docks. He could hear a horse's hooves clopping on the stone street and the creaking wheels of a rickety cart, but he not only couldn't see the confounded beast, he didn't even know which direction the driver was headed.

"I'm too old to have to put up with this," Hamish grumbled. "A man could catch pneumonia in this weather."

When the brick building with the sign Bucket of Ale loomed in front of him, Hamish mounted the three steps, pulled on the heavy door and entered the musty men's club. The log in the big fireplace kept the place somewhat warm.

Hamish slapped his arms against his sides, trying to put some warmth back in his chilled bones. He glanced around the richly furnished room. In the back, four of the wealthiest freight companies owners, Brody Hawkins, the youngest and richest of the lot, Casey Riggs, Otis Wooten and Lester Gilbert, were seated in deep leather chairs, enjoying their drinks and cigars.

Hamish made his way to the bar. Once he had a cup of hot rum in hand, he joined the four gentlemen.

"Tell me, Brody," a rotund man said, smoothing his thick moustache with a plumb finger, "do you think this year is going to be as profitable as last?"

Brody Hawkins leaned back in his chair and grinned. "Lester, as long as Horace Greeley wants to tell young men to go West, there can be nothing but more profit for all."

"If you can stop the Indian raids," Hamish interjected as he plunked down on a leather chair.

"Heard about your bad luck, Hamish," Lester said, "but you didn't lose everything. You can start over."

"Lost twenty men and half my shipment 'cause of them Injuns."

Brody studied the weathered man seated across from him. "Hamish, I told you I'd help you along until you're able to pay me back."

"I'm too old to start over. So, as of thirty minutes ago, I'm a retired man. Gonna move somewhere that's got warmer weather."

Otis chuckled, his slit of a mouth peeking from his thick beard. "It's plenty hot here in the summer."

Hamish sneered. "It ain't the summers I'm talkin' 'bout, Otis, and you know it."

A waiter came forward, asking if anyone wanted his drink refilled. Most of them shook their heads.

"If that's the way you feel, why don't I buy your wagons, Hamish?" Brody puffed on his cigar. "It's time I expanded my business."

Casey Riggs ran a big hand over his unruly red head. "At the rate you're going, Brody, you'll soon own every wagon on the Sante Fe and Oregon trails," he grumbled.

"Like I said, there's enough for everyone," Brody replied evenly.

"Well, you needn't worry about Brody getting richer with my wagons," Hamish spoke up. "Done sold my outfit to someone else already."

Brody's gaze touched each man. "All right, which one of you beat me to it?"

They all shook their heads before focusing their eyes on Hamish who was enjoying his rum.

"Well?" Casey asked impatiently. "You planning on answering the question or do you expect us to guess?"

"I can tell you that it'll do you no good poking questions. It ain't no one you know." Hamish licked his lips. Ever since the sale, he had been itching to break the news to the others.

"It's gotta be someone who lives in town, which means we know him," Casey insisted. "How else would he have known you wanted to sell? Hell, you didn't even give any of us a chance to make a bid!''

''For God sakes, Hamish, are you going to tell us the man's name?'' Casey asked again.

Hamish smiled and took another long sip. Not often did he have such an attentive audience. ''Sold it to an old friend's offspring. A lawyer out of Independence handled it. Didn't make much profit, but enough to take care of me in my twilight years.'' He finished his drink and stood. ''The new owner will be arriving in a couple of weeks.'' He tipped his hat, enjoying his private joke, then left the club, chuckling.

Brody shook his head and grinned. ''He probably sold his outfit for a fortune to some unsuspecting dandy who doesn't even know which end of a bull-whip to grab. He knew none of us were about to pay him some ridiculous price.''

The others agreed.

Two weeks later, Brody stood looking out the second floor window of the Hawkins and Associates building, enjoying a respite of sunshine. Though it was still cold, there were no clouds in the sky.

He glanced below just as a carriage pulled to a halt across the street in front of Hamish Goldman's old office. Brody straightened, trying to get a look at the man who climbed out of the vehicle, but at that very moment, a wagon passed, blocking his view.

By the time the wagon moved on, he only managed

to catch a glimpse of a purple skirt with frills and ribbons, and a matching hat partially hidden by a parasol. Undoubtedly the new owner's wife. The lady would do well to mind where she stepped, he thought. Even though it had stopped raining, the street was still wet, and a person still sank past his ankles in mud if he tried walking across it.

Brody turned back into his spacious office. He didn't have the time to stand around speculating. "I'll be back later," he informed his secretary as he left his office.

The thin man nodded, never taking his eyes from his work.

Brody went down the stairs and out the back of the building where he kept his saddle horse.

"Ain't it a fine day?" the young stable hand asked as he backed a big gray out of his stall.

"That it is, Henry. That it is."

As Brody swung up into the saddle, he decided that tomorrow afternoon he'd go over to Goodman's office and get acquainted with the new owner. He always liked to size up his competition.

Brody rode around the building and onto the main street. As he glanced to his left, he caught sight of a big, powerful man stepping out of Goodman's office. From the size of him, Brody assumed the new owner had worked as a teamster. But how much did he know about the other end of freighting?

Hamish's small carriage arrived as Brody continued on his way.

Sara automatically raised the hem of her velvet skirt as she scanned the dusty, cluttered room. There was so much grime on the window that the sunshine couldn't even peek through. "How long have you been closed down, Hamish?"

Hamish rushed forward. For two and a half weeks he'd prayed that nothing would go awry before she put her signature on the final papers. "Now if you're lookin' at the lay of the room, mouse—"

"From now on you will call me by my proper name, Sara, not by some foolish nickname."

"You sure you don't want me callin' you Miss Miles?"

"If you like."

Hamish spit tobacco juice in the spittoon. "As I started to say, you gotta remember I'm shut down during the winter."

Several weeks ago he had thought the sale final. H hadn't realized a clause had been inserted that allowed Sara to back out of the deal if she chose. Harold Miles's girl was a cautious woman.

Sara circled her hands around her waist. "There's still work to be done in the winter, Hamish."

"Now you know how yer pa hated it when you scolded…Sara. Besides, a little dirt only means something to a woman, not a man. But more important, when are you going to sign these papers I been holdin' so I can get my money? After all, wasn't I an old friend of your pa's? I'm askin' a fair price. Surely you don't think I'd be tryin' to take unfair advantage of you?"

Sara's soft peal of laughter bore no humor. "I don't think, I know." She turned to the big man patiently standing beside her. "Lucas, go to the wagon yards and take inventory. I'm anxious to find out what I'm about to buy and what condition it's in."

Lucas made Hamish nervous. The wagon master was entirely too silent for Hamish's liking. Even as Lucas went outside, his steps were as quiet as a cat's paws. But Sara's pa had said on more than one occasion that Lucas was going to make the best wagon master the West had ever seen.

Hamish sighed. "Well, I guess I'll go to the men's club and have a drink while you mosey through the ledgers."

"You'll do no such thing." Sara pulled a handkerchief from her reticule and tried dusting off the seat of the chair as best she could. She didn't even try to clean the rickety desk she sat behind. "You'll stay right here to answer any questions I might have. We also need to discuss your customers and suppliers. And starting tomorrow, you'll start introducing me to each of the buyers."

"But—"

Sara pursed her lips and narrowed her brown eyes.

Hamish had seen her give that same determined look to her father when he came home drunk. A man looking at that pretty, wide-eyed face probably thought Sara was a sweet dove who needed a man to take care of her and make the important decisions. But Hamish knew differently. He'd seen how her pa always ended up sleeping in one of the animal stalls until he sobered, no matter how much he protested.

Hamish sighed. Why fight it? Sara knew exactly what she wanted from him and he wasn't gonna be able to go to the Bucket of Ale until she got it. He pulled a chair over and sat.

Three days later, Sara finally signed the papers. Hamish was ecstatic, and so was Sara. Had Hamish misled her about the condition of his stock and wagons, she would have been in considerable trouble. She'd taken a big gamble when she'd bragged to Colonel Singleton about buying Hamish out and becoming a larger company.

The following week, Sara left town to complete the shipping of her goods to her new home.

Chapter Three

As they usually did before heading home, the four freighters sat in the rear of men's club, contemplating.

"I guess you've heard that Hamish sold his company to a woman." Casey waited for the waiter to serve drinks and hand out cigars before continuing. "He could have told us instead of letting us find out by way of the grapevine."

Otis Wooten nodded. "It's not unheard of for a female to own a freighting company or even work as a bullwhacker."

"But it's damn rare." Casey lit his cigar.

Brody shook his head. "It came as a shock to me. I thought it was that big ramrod of a man I saw. I would have known differently if I hadn't been so busy and had gone over there like I planned." He shoved back a tuft of black hair that had fallen onto his forehead. "I saw Hamish the other day. He's still acting secretive. I asked him where the new owner learned the trade. All Hamish would say was, 'What difference does it make?'''

Otis Wooten chuckled. "He's got a point."

"What's he keeping under his hat?" Casey speculated.

"I'll tell you what I think." Brody sipped his glass of port. "I'll wager the woman in question knows nothing about what she's getting herself into."

"I'd say she's a widow," Otis suggested. "Some sweet, timid woman he's regaled with tales of great wealth. 'Course he undoubtedly left out the part about the hardships. All along the crafty old buzzard planned to continue running the place himself. All he needed was her money."

If Brody Hawkins didn't have meetings with bankers, suppliers or customers, he could be found in his office, keeping an eye on the closed door across the street. He wanted to see the woman Hamish had hogswallowed.

Brody had just moved to the window when the lady in question stepped from her buggy and entered the building. Had Hamish found her somewhere out on the prairie? Her face was hidden, but she had to be along in years, judging by her old-fashioned gown with frills and ribbons, and the ridiculous matching hat and parasol. And even had she been dressed in a more suitable manner, she gave the impression of a lady going to a tea instead of running a freight company.

Brody slowly shook his head. Hamish had to have been in his cups when he'd sworn the lady would steal business from the others. Otis's assumption that Hamish intended to continue running the freight company seemed accurate.

"I have some papers for you to sign, Mr. Hawkins."

Brody turned and looked at the gray-haired clerk. "I'm going across the way. I'll do it when I come back."

Brody dropped his partially smoked cigar in the cuspidor.

"Hamish seems to have found some foolish woman who wants to give her money away," Brody commented.

"He's got a new wagon master named Lucas Collier," said Dusty, a bull of a man going over shipment orders. "Mule skinners that come upriver have spoken of him." He frowned. "Hear tell he's mighty good at what he does and well worth his $125 a month."

Brody looked back out the window, a slight smile tugging at the corners of his mouth. The lady had a right to know she was being taken advantage of. Had she actually bought the company? If so, maybe he should offer to pay back her investment.

"I'm going to meet my new competitor." He left the room and started down the stairs in a gingerly manner.

Dusty chuckled softly. "No one can say the boss

ever let an opportunity slip from between his fingers. He's out to get Hamish's company and a new wagon master.''

''Whatever he's up to isn't any of our business,'' the clerk stated firmly. ''Now let's continue going through these supply orders.''

Sara glanced around at the dark, dismal office. Slowly she removed the two hat pins then carefully sat her hat aside. A fresh coat of paint, curtains and a picture or two on the walls would make a vast improvement. Admittedly her small business didn't begin to compare to Hawkins and Associates across the street, but it was a start in the right direction.

She had every intention of making sure Miles Freighting grew. Thanks to her departed father and brother, she had a lot of contacts, all of which she intended to utilize. She'd already set up a line of credit with the bank for purchases, stock, wages and provisions, something that most banks disallowed women. Her army contract had been a big influence on the bank's decision.

''Hello?'' a deep voice called from out front. ''Anyone here?''

Sara quickly slipped from behind her desk and hurried through the doorway that adjoined the two rooms. A tall, broad-shouldered man had his back turned to her. ''I apologize for the lack of help, but my clerks…''

As the man turned and faced her, Sara stopped breathing. His perfectly fitted waistcoat and trousers, starched white shirt and properly trimmed goatee indicated a businessman...and undoubtedly a man to be reckoned with. On the other hand, his sun-darkened skin, the lack of perfumed macassar oil in his black, wind-tossed hair, and his sea-green eyes somehow belied that business appearance. Or was it his lean, chiseled features and easy smile that gave a hint of an adventurer? With the right attire, he'd be the perfect pirate who wildly raided ships and carried beautiful, willing damsels off to sea.

"You were saying?"

"Oh, yes. I mean..." Had she been staring? She cleared her throat and tried again. "As I started to say, my clerks won't arrive until the day after tomorrow." It was sinful that a man should be so handsome. Handsome? No, *handsome* wasn't the right word. Dangerous...rugged...virile...suited him better. "What can I do for you?"

Brody laughed inwardly at the question. Though tempted, he didn't say what first came to mind. "Allow me to introduce myself. The name is Brody Hawkins—"

"Of Hawkins & Associates?" Did he hear her heart pounding?

"Then you've heard of me?"

"Who hasn't? You're one of the partners across the street."

"There are no partners. I just liked the sound of it."
What was there about Hamish that had attracted some-
one so young and naive? Brody wondered. "I thought
I'd be neighborly and welcome the new owner of—"

"Miles Freighting. The sign will be raised tomorrow. Won't you come into my office? It's a bit
cleaner."

Brody followed her into the next room. "Then
you're not going to keep Hamish's name?" He could
never recall having seen a woman with silver-blond
hair and big brown eyes.

"Good gracious, no. Why would I do that?"

"Why, indeed? Mrs. Miles—"

"It's Miss Miles."

Brody scratched the back of his head. So far he'd
been a hundred percent wrong about everything, except one. A woman so petite with such full, kissable
lips, ample bosom and tiny waist was far more suited
for pleasuring men than trying to act the business-
woman.

How could the woman possibly know a single thing
about freighting? How she'd gotten the fort contracts
was beyond anything he could imagine. Unless... No,
Colonel Singleton was too smart to set aside something that important for a woman's wiles.

"Miss Miles, I'll get right down to business. I never
liked seeing someone being swindled. Therefore I'm
willing to purchase your company at its valued price."

Sara was shocked by the offer. "Why?"

"As I said, I don't like seeing anyone being swindled, especially a young, beautiful woman as yourself."

"But—" His raised hand silenced her.

"I know Hamish weaves a good story, but believe me, Miss Miles, the freighting business is no place for a lady of your—"

"My what?"

"Of your obvious delicate nature."

"I see."

"May I sit?"

It suddenly occurred to her that he wanted to put her out of business! "Forgive my lack of manners," she said in a friendly voice. Two could place his game of mock concern. "Please, do have a seat." Sara motioned to the dirtier of two chairs then took her place behind her desk.

His face set in granite, Brody leaned forward and looked deeply into the lady's magnificent brown eyes. If he played his cards right, he'd be able to purchase everything for less than Hamish would have wanted.

"I don't know how much you paid Hamish, but I'm certain it was more than his holdings were worth. I can't pay all your money back, but I'm willing to take everything off your hands at a fair price. More important, you'll be assured of not losing more money on a hopeless venture."

"How magnanimous of you, Mr. Hawkins." Sara considered calling him a number of choice names, but chose to hear what other gestures he might make. When working for her father, she had dealt with many such men.

Sara fingered one of the tails of the crimson ribbon tied around the lacy neck of her blouse. He was very sure of himself. "Your offer is most kind, but I believe I can make a very nice income off of Miles Freighting."

"To be successful in any endeavor requires knowledge and hard work. I'm sure you would be far better suited for another occupation. You're much too pretty to dirty such dainty hands."

"Are you insinuating what I think—"

"I'm not insinuating anything. I'm simply trying to point out the hardships your undertaking involves." He leaned forward. "Perhaps I should demonstrate what I'm talking about. You need reliable wagons, stock, equipment and drivers. What is your wagon master doing right now?"

Sara's cheeks burned. "What are your wagon masters doing?"

"That's a moot point."

"Then just what is the point?"

"I'm trying to show you how you're going to lose your money on an unwise investment." He shoved the chair back and stood.

If Sara hadn't been so angry she probably would have laughed at seeing so big a man moving about in such a small room.

"Where are you going to get the commodities to transport? You'll need more than the fort contracts to keep you going."

Sara slowly stood, her hands balled into fists. "I want to be sure I understand what you are proposing. Are you offering to help me with your expertise?"

"I'm offering to help by buying you out. You'll never get the financial backing you need," he assured her.

"Forgive me. When you said you're only thinking of my welfare, I assumed you wanted to help me succeed," Sara deliberately chided. She walked to the edge of the desk and leaned against it. "But since that's not your intention, what I'm doing is none of your business. When I bought Hamish's company, I knew exactly what I was doing and the value of his assets."

Sara moved a little closer to the towering man. "And don't try telling me I'm a woman, therefore I'm incapable of making money from this endeavor. I've heard such comments all my life." She took a deep breath. "I'll be running three outfits, Mr. Hawkins. As you are aware, it takes roughly five hundred thousand dollars to put together twenty-five wagons, wages and provisions, but the estimated gross is nine hundred forty-five thousand. No, Mr. Hawkins, I have no intentions of selling to you or anyone else. If there is nothing else you care to discuss, please leave."

Taken off guard by her knowledge, Brody slowly

walked to the doorway. "Let me know when you change your mind."

Not since he was a young boy had anyone had the nerve to order him out. Yet there stood a wink of a woman no more than five foot two in stature, breasts shoved out in indignation—very nice breasts at that—doing just that.

Brody stopped and turned, his lopsided grin masking his irritation. "We'll see if you're of the same mind six months down the road. The offer might still be there if you have anything left to sell. Naturally the buying price will be considerably lower."

Brody left the room. If their livelihood depended on character analysis, he, Otis, Lester and Casey would be flat broke. They should have listened when Hamish said he'd sold the business to an offspring of a friend of his.

A light suddenly turned on in his mind. Hadn't she said her name was Miles? And wasn't that the name of the small freighting company who'd had the Army contracts last? That couldn't be a coincidence. Had the company been hers, her father's, or had it belonged to some relative?

Sara slammed her right fist down on the top of the desk, then grabbed her hand with the other one in an effort to alleviate the pain. She then collapsed onto the nearest chair. If only she'd had something to throw at the insufferable man!

Hawkins hadn't been the first man she'd locked horns with when it came to freighting, and he undoubtedly wouldn't be the last. But somehow she'd hoped his attitude would be different. Unthinkingly, she began tapping a staccato on top of the desk with her fingernails.

It always made her angry to meet up with narrow-minded men. It also made her all the more determined to prove them wrong.

Once again she was fighting for respectability in a field dominated by men. Well, Mr. Hawkins and others were in for a surprise. She hadn't given up when she was young and she wasn't about to do it now. She'd show the illustrious Mr. Brody Hawkins she did not have to forgo her femininity to run a freighting company.

Sara's face suddenly blossomed. Mr. Hawkins had been shocked when she'd rattled off monetary amounts. He was going to be downright angry when she started taking business away from him. Contacts and flair accomplished many things.

That evening at the men's club, Brody relaxed and enjoyed a brandy while answering his fellow businessmen's questions.

"Well?" Otis asked. "What's she like?"

"A mighty fine-looking woman who is in need of a man's guidance," Brody replied.

"Is it true she took the fort contract right out from

under your nose?'' Otis Wooten asked, his bird eyes twinkling with humor.

"Not really,'' Brody answered calmly, although it irritated the hell out of him that she *had* literally snatched it out of his hands. "It's of minor significance and I'll get it eventually.''

He'd decided not to say anything about the likelihood of her family being the previous shippers.

Casey Riggs frowned. "My wife saw Sara Miles at a soiree a few weeks back, escorted by the very same Colonel who gave her those contracts. According to Patricia, the lady flirted outrageously with a senator from Washington. Patricia said he was old enough to be Miss Miles's father, but the senator obviously enjoyed every minute of her attention. Patricia was quite fervent about not allowing that type to attend functions given by decent folks.''

Brody chuckled. "Miss Miles seems to have already become the talk of Leavenworth.''

"We'd better start watching our rears, gentlemen,'' Casey stated. "The next thing we know she'll be taking contracts from all of us.''

Chapter Four

Sara stuck a silk red rose in her hair and looked in the mirror. She liked the way the rose offset the royal-blue ball gown she'd had made especially for this occasion.

If her father could have seen her now, he'd have locked her in her room and thrown away the key. A mental picture of him flashed through her mind. He had always been overly protective and had insisted she be dressed properly. He believed nice girls wore dresses that came to their chins, covered the arms and had lots of lace and ruffles.

Now here she stood, a tiny bit of lace, no ruffles, and looking like one of the Angels of the Night she'd heard about. She tugged at the neckline, but the dress didn't budge. Though the seamstress had insisted that a low décolletage was fashionable, Sara had demanded lace be inserted. Mrs. Brady had complied, but with as little as possible. The swell of her breasts was still too obvious. But there was nothing to be done about it now.

Sara glanced at the invitation resting on her chest of drawers. She still found it hard to believe that Brody Hawkins had invited her to his winter ball. The gesture had left her suspicious. He probably hadn't expected her to accept. He had thought wrong. She wasn't about to refuse such an opportunity. Perhaps she'd meet someone who would deliver future contracts to her company. Besides, having lived a simple life, this was the first invitation she'd ever had to so prestigious an affair.

Though her family eventually became financially secure, her father had insisted they remain living in the same area and the same house they'd occupied since before she'd been born. People probably thought they were as poor as church mice, since her pa had been very frugal when it came to money.

She reached for the elbow-length gloves lying on the bed, then took one last look in the mirror. Convinced she could do nothing more, she grabbed the ermine-lined cape her erstwhile fiancé had given her as a gift a year ago. She'd been thrilled, until she'd found out that he'd bought it with her money.

She walked to the window and pulled back the curtain. Mr. Hawkins's coach had arrived.

It wasn't until the driver brought the coach to a halt in front of a stately brick mansion that Sara began having second thoughts. She had expected a fancy house, but not a building three stories tall. She wasn't about to try counting all the windows with candlelight spilling from them. Coming had been a mistake. A brazen act to think she could mingle with the wealthy. She was more like a gnawed corncob being tossed into a field of orchids!

Sara jumped when the coachman opened the door. It was too late to go back home. Her knees shaking, she automatically took his hand and let him help her from the coach. At least she didn't fall and make a fool of herself.

Get control, Sara silently chastised. You can not…will not…allow such grandeur to intimidate you. You're as good as anyone here.

Sara counted each of the ten steps she ascended. Her eyes fixed on the doorman waiting to open the huge front door. She gave him a hesitant smile before stepping inside, her lips forming an O as she looked around the large foyer. It actually had a marble floor and the beautiful decor defied description.

Again she wanted to turn and run, but her determination strengthened when she realized that in a couple of years—assuming everything went as planned—she could also live in such grandeur.

''This way, madam.''

The servant led Sara into the magnificent ballroom. It had to be some sort of dream. A full orchestra sat on the balcony while beautiful people graced the lower level. The women's gowns created a kaleidoscope of rich colors and the candlelight on their jewelry created a sea of glittering light. Her seamstress had been correct. Most of the gowns the women wore plunged much lower than hers. But she still felt naked. Weren't the women afraid their breasts would fall out if they leaned forward?

As she looked around the long room, it occurred to Sara that she didn't recognize a single face. What was she to do? Stand in one spot all night?

"I don't believe we've met."

Sara hadn't seen the suave gentleman approaching.

"My name is Curtis Farmington. I know we haven't met. I could never forget such beauty."

The compliment boosted Sara's confidence. "You're right. We haven't met." Though grateful that he had saved her from an embarrassing situation, her misgivings were suddenly overpowering. She turned, ready to depart, but the young gentleman took her hand.

"I hope you're not planning on leaving. We should get acquainted. Why don't we start with a dance?"

Across the room, Brody detached an attractive brunette's arm from his and started making his way toward where Sara Miles stood. At first he hadn't recognized her. This was an entirely different woman than the one he had met previously. The bodice of her gown fit like a second glove with yards of material gathered and draped behind her. There were no bows and frills. The woman waiting to descend the wide stairs was a perfect work of art, and he did so like to collect art.

Seeing Curtis escort Sara onto the dance floor, Brody paused and allowed his eyes the pleasure of looking at her. A picture of beauty and grace, he thought, until he saw her stumble over Curtis's foot a couple of times. The lady was either very nervous, hadn't danced much, or both, which surprised him. After hearing about her prowess with a bullwhip from the colonel at the fort, he'd begun to wonder if there was anything she couldn't do. No doubt about it, the lady had guts.

Brody made his way onto the floor and tapped Curtis's shoulder. Curtis's look made it clear that he didn't appreciate having to relinquish his partner, but he finally gave way to protocol.

Brody took Sara into his arms and proceeded to lead her around the floor.

"Thank you for inviting me tonight," Sara said stiffly, her heart having moved to her throat.

"Take a deep breath and relax."

"I beg your pardon?" She resented the subtle mockery in his tone.

"I said, take a deep breath and relax. You're as tight as a wagon spring and you've already stepped on my feet twice."

"Of all the nerve," Sara said defensively. "No gentleman would accuse a lady of such a thing."

"I've never claimed to be a gentleman."

No, a pirate, Sara thought.

"Why are you in a huff?" Brody inquired. "It's my feet that are being trodden upon. You're supposed to let me lead while you listen to the rhythm of the music. It's one, two, three...one, two, three. No, no. Don't look at your feet."

Sara wished she had her bullwhip. She'd show him how to dance.

"Look in my eyes and listen to the music."

"Don't be silly. How is that going to help?" She tripped over his foot again and would have fallen had he not held her up. "I've had enough!" To her chagrin, he continued dancing as if she hadn't said a word. "Did you hear what I said?" Sara asked.

"I heard. Are you afraid to look into my eyes?"

Sara looked up. "Don't be ridiculous." She looked away just as she again stepped on his toes. A quick glance around the floor convinced her no one had noticed. "See?" she said angrily. "It accomplished nothing. Now if you would—"

"You shouldn't have looked away," he replied calmly. "You don't strike me as a woman who gives up so easily. Or perhaps being the focus of gossip doesn't bother you."

"What are you talking about?"

"Didn't you know that the wives of the town's wealthy and powerful men believe you to be—how can I put it delicately—they do not consider you a lady of morals.''

"What?'' She looked around the edge of the dance floor and saw both younger and older women talking behind their fans. Were they discussing her?

Fighting the sting of tears in her eyes, Sara again tried to pull away. As before, her effort was futile. "Is this why you invited me? Am I to be the entertainment for the evening? Let me go, or I warn you, I'll really give them something to talk about.''

"What's wrong, sweetheart? Can't you take a challenge?''

"I can handle a challenge as well as any other—''

"Man?''

"That's not what I was going to say.''

Brody smiled. "Yes, it was. From what I hear, you're very adept at handling men, but what about women?''

Sara wondered how much longer she was going to have to put up with this. Would the music never stop?

"I dare you to show the ladies watching that you know the social art of dancing.'' Brody felt her chest rise from indignation.

"I do know how to dance, but not to this music!''

"Then look into my eyes and listen,'' he commanded. "It's called a waltz.''

Determined to show him this wasn't going to work, Sara looked him straight in the eye. When had she suddenly become lost in that sea of green? She was vaguely aware of the music as she floated around the floor in his arms. All else faded from her mind...until she realized she was standing still and the music had stopped.

"See," Brody said, his lips spreading in a knowing smile, "it always works better if you let the man lead."

Sara wanted to rub his smug face in cow dung. He had not only proven his point, he'd known exactly what her reaction would be. "That's debatable. Perhaps now you will escort me off the dance floor. I'm a bit out of breath."

He openly appraised her with his eyes, momentarily pausing at the rise of her breasts. "You look in fine condition to me. Or are you so fragile that you can't manage just one more dance?"

The orchestra started playing again.

Though he hadn't spoken the words, the devilish glint in his eyes made it perfectly clear he'd just issued a dare. "Very well." She felt warm again when he took her in his arms. "What is all this about?"

"I don't understand your question."

"Why did you invite me tonight? Why are you taking the trouble to dance with me? You'll never convince me to sell."

"You have a suspicious nature. Why can't you just accept it as a friendly gesture to a very attractive lady?"

"Did you know I took another contract from you?"

"If you're referring to the patent reaper and mower, the steam engine and boiler, together with all the machinery necessary for a new flouring mill, yes. I knew about it and I thank you."

"What do you mean you thank me?"

"It was a contract that wasn't brought to my attention. The man no longer works for me."

"I don't believe you!"

"Ask any of the other freighters I tried to get to haul it to Santa Fe. My dear, Hawkins and Associates is far too large for you to do any damage." He looked down and grinned. "Though I find your efforts entertaining, I do think you'd be wise to accept my offer then settle down with a husband and family."

He turned her in a wide circle and when Sara stepped on his foot this time, it was deliberate.

"We're really going to have to work on the turns," Brody said dryly.

When the music stopped, Brody took Sara's elbow and led her off the dance floor. He nodded or made a brief comment to those they passed, but he didn't come to a halt until they were standing in front of four elderly women, seated on regal high-backed chairs.

"Ladies," he greeted.

Sara was becoming familiar with his devilish grin.

"As I promised, I am placing Miss Miles in your capable hands. I'm sure you already know that she is a new resident of Leavenworth. Miss Miles, these lovely ladies are known as the Baronesses of Kansas."

When he made the introductions, Sara recognized three of the women's last names. Their sons were her competitors. After what Brody had said about the wealthy women accusing her of loose morals, Sara was surprised to see the interest on the elderly women's creased faces.

"We've been dying to meet you," Nallie Wooten said in her raspy voice.

"Bertha," Clara Riggs said, "slide over a chair so Miss Miles can sit between us."

"Miss Miles, I leave you in the best of hands." Brody smiled. "You couldn't ask for better company."

The ladies giggled. Sara sat in the chair they had vacated for her.

As soon as Brody turned away, the older women began talking.

"Miss Miles, we watched you dancing with Brody. You turn a fine toe."

Apparently they hadn't seen her stumbling about. "Please call me Sara."

"Brody is the most eligible man in town, you know."

"Why shouldn't he be? He's not only rich, he's devastatingly handsome," Nallie spoke up.

"I think he's taken a special interest in my granddaughter."

"I doubt that, Bertha," Clara said. "It's more like

wishful thinking on both your parts. He treats all women as if they were special, including us.''

''My grandson is single and very eligible,'' Harriet told Sara.

''But not as eligible as Brody,'' Nallie stated.

The women were talking so fast that Sara kept turning her head from one side to the other.

''I'm not interested in finding a man,'' Sara spoke up. ''As for Mr. Hawkins, he may be handsome, but he's absolutely not anyone I would be interested in.''

Clara flipped open her lace fan and began fanning herself. ''I imagine you're wondering why we wanted to talk to you?''

Sara only had time enough to nod.

Bertha leaned forward. ''It's been a long time since anyone with spunk has made as big a stir in town, and we wanted to meet you. Believe me, it can get downright boring when you reach our age.''

Clara cleared her throat. ''My daughter-in-law, Patricia Riggs, is not only the biggest snob in Kansas, she is also the biggest gossip. We wanted to find out if what she's been saying is true. Are you indeed a woman of loose morals?''

''You certainly don't look like one,'' Bertha Kestrel commented. ''You and Brody were such a beautiful couple on the dance floor.''

''Hush,'' Clara admonished, ''you don't even know what a loose woman looks like.''

''I certainly do!''

Sara was shocked by their bluntness. A thought suddenly occurred to her. "Did one of you ask Brody Hawkins to invite me tonight?"

"Of course," Harriet replied.

Clara chuckled. "And my daughter-in-law has been having an absolute fit from the moment you walked into the room."

"Please, dear, tell us about yourself," Clara said kindly. "Is it true that you've opened your own freight company?"

"Ah, yes." Sarah was still trying to accept the strangeness of it all. Though tempted to leave, she settled into her chair. Apparently these women wielded a very heavy hand. Why else would Brody heed their request? She'd stay and see what developed. "My father was a freighter," she said with a wide smile.

Chapter Five

Sara entered the front office of Miles Freighting and quickly glanced around. Though she hadn't seen Brody Hawkins since the ball a few weeks ago, she'd had a notion that he'd be waiting for her arrival.

"Are there any messages?" she asked her clerk.

He handed her two pieces of paper, both notes from Lucas. Sara continued on into her office. She didn't need a man in her life now. So why did she keep thinking about Brody? Because he'd danced with her?

Sara plopped down in her chair and looked at the pile of papers on her desk. The stack never got smaller. She needed to hire another clerk. She glanced around the room with unseeing eyes. Why couldn't she rid herself of the sensation of being lost in the depths of his green eyes?

Determined to work, she opened the ledger. The carefully scripted numbers glared up at her, bringing a smile. The senator had returned to Washington, but he hadn't forgotten their conversation at the fort. People were looking to invest their money with the hopes of high yields in the freighting industry. She already had contracts and when the ice broke at the point of Saint Louis and the boats started making their way upriver, she'd be sending out three teams consisting of twenty wagons each. Before long, she'd be a rich woman. If only her pa and brother were here to see what she had accomplished.

Sara suddenly felt lonely. It still hurt when she thought of the loss of her family. She no longer had anyone to share her happiness and sorrows with except the Baronesses, who had so graciously taken her under their wings. She loved having tea with the elderly women when she could manage to slip away. Never having known her mother, she rather liked being fussed and watched over. On three occasions they had actually sent complete meals to her office with notes stating she was too thin and worked too hard.

Across the street, Brody also sat at his desk going through the list of orders still to be filled. "Come in," he called upon hearing a knock at his door.

A short, unimposing man entered, his hat held in one hand and papers in the other.

"Ah, William King," Brody greeted, but didn't bother to stand. "Have a seat. Have you the information?"

The neatly dressed man smiled. "I have."

"Well?"

King placed his hat on the desk. "The information wasn't hard to come by," he said as soon as he was seated. "Seems everyone in Atchison knew the family. They were well liked and honest."

"Get on with it," Brody stated impatiently.

"Well, Harold Miles and his son, Edmond, had a profitable little freighting business. But a little over a year ago they were both killed instantly when a loaded wagon overturned on them. Do you want the particulars?"

"Anything suspicious about the wagon turning over?"

"No, it—"

"Then continue on."

"The two men enjoyed their liquor and raised a bit of hell occasionally. They watched over the daughter and sister, Sara Rose Miles, whom they called mouse—"

"Mouse?"

"Yes, sir. Anyhow, they watched over the girl with such tenacity that when she grew older, no man dared come courting. But I found no gossip of interest about any of them until Malcolm Speck came onto the scene."

Brody leaned back in his chair.

"Word is that Sara Miles, who ran the business end of the small freighting company, took the loss of her father and brother badly. Folks said she was inconsolable, until a man named Malcolm Speck stepped into her life. Seems Miss Miles and Speck were engaged at one time.''

William King flipped through his handwritten notes to be sure the next name was correct. ''A Mrs. Cutter said Miss Miles was so lonely after the loss of her family that she was 'an egg waiting to be hatched. Then that rooster Speck came upon the scene.' Her words, not mine, sir. He was worldly and she had led a sheltered life. The swindler recognized a waiting target, as the woman put it. She said Sara changed completely after meeting Speck. She became more of a lady than a tomboy.

Brody thought of the beautiful woman waiting on the steps of the ballroom. He had seen her rough edges and only hints of gracefulness. Now he knew why. She hadn't had a mother to help polish and refine her.

''Neighbors said she really blossomed until one day she discovered Speck had taken off with most of her inheritance.'' Mr. Hawkins's expression gave no indication as to whether or not King had obtained the information the powerful man wanted.

''How did Speck manage that?''

''No one seems to know.''

''What did Miss Miles do after Speck left?''

''Went into seclusion and refused to talk to anyone.''

''And where is Mr. Speck now?''

"No one knows that, either. He hasn't been seen or heard from since."

"Were Speck and Miss Miles lovers?"

"Everyone assumed so. He had moved into the house with her. Mrs. Cutter also commented that the girl's father would turn over in his grave if he knew what had gone on in his home."

"Anything else?"

King shook his head. "That's it. If you like, I'll see if I can locate Speck."

"That won't be necessary." Brody reached into a drawer, pulled out some money and tossed it onto the desk. "You've supplied me with all I needed to know."

Brody watched King pick up his pay, stand, then silently leave the room.

As soon as the door closed, Brody stood and walked to the window. The broom-tail horse and buggy parked in front of Miles Freighting told him that Sara was at work. Thoughtfully, he rubbed the side of his chin. Had he investigated Sara's life for business purposes or personal reasons? Probably both. Some of the other freighters were getting antsy about the business she had already taken from them and he was getting tired of being teased about losing the fort contracts.

Brody turned away from the window. The lady certainly hadn't let any grass grow under her feet. She had managed to tap into just about everyone's business. She may not have the polish other women possessed, but she was clever.

In an effort to obtain business, she wasn't above flirting with potential customers. But from everything he'd heard, she always managed to avoid fulfilling the hinted promises of a more personal nature. Even knowing that, men continued to give her business in hopes that he might be the one she eventually favored.

Brody chuckled. He'd had a few fantasies about the lady himself, and had given more than a little thought about taking her to bed. A few years ago he'd have enjoyed the challenge and done exactly that. But Sara had bonded with the Baronesses. And his plans for the future were already in place. They weren't going to be changed by dallying with Miss Miles.

The wily woman didn't know it, but he was doing her a favor by staying away. He had a habit of quickly tiring of his conquests. Besides, she'd had enough happen to her in the last year without him stepping into her life.

On the other side of town, a straight-backed, tightly-corseted woman walked into a small, two-story house. As she entered the musty parlor, she held a lace handkerchief to her nose. The room was so cluttered with furniture and memorabilia that there was hardly enough room to walk, let alone sit.

"How can you abide living in such squalor," Patricia complained as she shoved some knitting to the side, allowing her a spot on the edge of the sofa. "Have your servants air this place out and throw most of this stuff away."

"You'll learn some day that age has a way of making things more precious," the elderly woman seated in the comfortable armchair replied.

Patricia frowned. "You sent your houseboy with a message that you wanted to see me."

"That I do."

"Well, please get on with it. I have a lot of errands to attend to."

"For the big lawn party you're giving next week?"

"That's right." Seeing her reflection in the diamond glass mirror, Patricia adjusted her wide hat a little to the right, then pinched her cheeks for color. "You still haven't said whether you'll be there or not."

Clara Riggs resented her daughter-in-law's haughtiness. She looked down at her hands. When had they become so wrinkled? "Is Sara Miles invited?"

Patricia jumped to her feet, her eyes flashing. "Certainly not!"

"Sit down!"

Patricia dropped back onto the sofa.

"I want you to befriend Sara Miles. The girl is in need of a little polish. Something you are very good at."

"I'll do no such thing! She's a whore!"

"I thought you would react like that. Nevertheless, the Baronesses—"

Patricia sneered. "Baronesses, bah. Why do you persist in calling yourselves that?"

"Being four of the most influential women in the Kansas Territory—and Missouri—we can call ourselves anything we damn well like. At Brody's ball the other week, I saw exactly why you do not like Sara and why you don't want her anywhere around."

"I don't make a habit of befriending that type of person."

"Of course not. With her around you're no longer the belle of the ball. You should be happy for what you have and be busy making a good home for Casey and your children. But instead you run around behind his back with other men. I admit you're good at hiding your affairs, but I have eyes everywhere—people who do not want me as an enemy. Casey's to blame, also. He should work less and pay more attention to his family. I have no idea as to whether he knows about your lovers or whether he chooses to not see what you're up to. Nevertheless, I do."

Seeing her mother-in-law was a bit riled, Patricia chose a different approach. "Clara, dear, think about what you're asking. Surely you don't want your son's wife to become the laughingstock of Leavenworth? My social standing helps his business and makes money for all of us."

"I don't care about money. I already have more than I'll spend in my lifetime."

"But you have to think of your darling grandchildren."

"My grandchildren are spoiled rotten and I never see them. You won't be made to look the fool when you explain to your so-called friends that you had been wrong about Sara and you feel obligated to prove what a nice person she is."

Patricia rose to her feet again. "No! I will never do such a thing! Nor can you make me! I refuse to listen to another word." She headed for the door.

"What will you do when you no longer have a home, fine clothes..."

Patricia paused.

"...and food in your larder?"

Patricia slowly turned. "You wouldn't."

"Oh, yes I would. I own over three-quarters of everything my son has and I have the power to put you out on your bottom. I've never kept how I feel about you a secret. The worst mistake my son ever made was to marry you."

Clara pulled her shawl around her shoulders. "Maybe you're from the East and know manners and such, but I came from Kentucky. I know what it is to do without. Don't get me wrong. I'm not complaining. It taught me to be grateful for what I have. Something you needed to learn a long time ago." Clara clasped her hands. "But it's never too late for you to start."

Patricia raised the hem of her green-and-gold striped skirt before resuming her place on the sofa.

Clara smiled sweetly. "Now that we understand each other, I'll tell you exactly what I want from you. You will take Sara in hand and teach her proper dress and decorum. Also..."

Though it was nearing dusk by the time Brody arrived at the Riggs's lawn party, everyone seemed to still be enjoying themselves. Some were even playing croquet in the fading light, another group was singing. He stopped and stared at Sara Miles. Since Patricia had tagged Sara a whore, why had she invited the woman? And Sara looked happy! The singing group hit a high note and Brody's jaw dropped. Patricia Riggs had actually placed her arm around Sara's shoulders and even smiled down at the smaller woman.

Totally confused, Brody moved to the table with food, most of which had already been consumed. He was about to take a bite of a finger sandwich when a big hand slapped him on the back.

"Glad you came," Casey Riggs blurted out.

Brody turned and smiled at his host who, from the smell of his breath and the redness of his eyes, had already imbibed in a bit too much.

"Just out of curiosity, why are you here?" Casey asked. "Personally I'd rather be at the club than attending one of these infernal things, but you know how Patricia loves to entertain."

Brody laugh was scornful. "I didn't want Patricia

nagging me for not making an appearance. I hadn't planned on staying long." He finished off his sandwich and reached for another. "I'm surprised to see Sara Miles here."

They both looked toward the group still singing. Brody liked the new way Sara's blond hair was pulled back and tied with a big ribbon. Darned if she didn't have the thickest eyelashes he'd ever seen. They made those big brown eyes shine like stars. Even her clothes were more stylish.

"I, too, was shocked." Casey grabbed a couple of sandwiches off the big platter then stared at them. "I don't know what Patricia thinks is so great about these little cucumber sandwiches. You can eat a dozen of them and still feel like you haven't eaten a thing."

"The petit fours look good," Brody pointed out. "I thought Patricia didn't like Sara."

"My wife is unpredictable. Now Patricia can't seem to do enough for the lady. Patricia's even introduced Miss Miles to all her friends, and is teaching the young lady to play the piano as well as the latest dance steps. Knowing Patricia she's probably also working on Sara's dress and mannerisms. I think she's trying to get the girl married off."

Casey popped a sandwich in his mouth. "Patricia is determined to introduce her protégée to every eligible male of good standing. As pretty as she is, she'll soon have them all chasing after her." Casey put one of the sandwiches back on the platter. "Why don't we go in and have a drink?"

Later, when Brody came back outside, he saw Sara surrounded by three men, one being Harriet Gilbert's grandson, Donald. Were the Baronesses trying to arrange something?

Brody went in search of Patricia to thank her for the invitation, and hopefully leave.

Sara hadn't been aware of Brody's arrival until she saw him walk out of the house. Being almost a head taller than most of the men, he wasn't hard to spot. At one point she would have sworn he was watching her. Had he noticed her new blouse and skirt or the way Patricia had styled her hair?

"Miss Miles, have you heard a thing I've said?"

Sara smiled at Donald Gilbert, the charmer of the group. "Of course I have, but would you mind repeating it?"

Donald and the other gentlemen laughed.

Out the corner of her eye, Sara saw the Quigley sisters joining Brody. Though the twins were attractive, Sara doubted that they had one brain between them. It was disgusting how they chased him. Didn't they have any pride? She would never... Why was she even thinking about him?

Sara didn't see Brody after that. He must have left and the twins were gone as well. Had he taken the women with him? The rest of the evening didn't seem quite as enjoyable.

* * *

As the days and weeks passed, Sara dove whole-heartedly into learning to be a lady. No matter what time she arrived home, she faithfully spent one hour walking with a book on her head before going to bed. She gloried at being involved in the social whirl, the likes of which she'd never known. Eligible men had popped up from nowhere, flirting and vying for her attention.

Secretly she called herself the belle of Kansas. Patricia referred to her as the butterfly of winter. Sara felt especially blessed at having such wonderful friends as the Baronesses and Patricia.

Sara wasn't certain as to when she began to notice Brody Hawkins's avoidance of her at social affairs, but once it came to her attention she wondered why she hadn't noticed it sooner.

Mr. Hawkins's obvious ostracism soon took on the annoyance of a pesky mosquito. She'd been told that he'd given two suppers, neither of which she'd been invited to. Admittedly she and Mr. Hawkins had never shared anything more than a few words; nevertheless he could have afforded an occasional nod of acknowledgement! Hadn't he noticed how much she had changed?

Yet, even after the way he acted, and more often than she cared to admit, his green eyes invaded her thoughts. She actually wasted an entire hour one day picturing herself being held by his strong arm as the black-haired swashbuckler, laughing in the wind, stole her from one ship and delivered her to another by way of a swinging rope.

Eventually, curiosity became partners with her anger. Why did the great Mr. Hawkins persist in ignoring her? She'd now fallen into the small group of women that he hadn't escorted one place or another. Did he believe the story about her being a woman of loose morals? The question was immediately dismissed. Though she knew very little about the man, she knew instinctively that he did not allow others to interfere in his life.

Why was he doing this? Because she'd taken more business from him? Because she wasn't born with a golden spoon in her mouth? Because she wasn't interesting? How would he know? They'd hardly spoken.

Sara finally decided to consult Patricia about the situation. They were sitting in the sunroom of Patricia's house when Sara approached the subject.

"Patricia, have you noticed that Mr. Hawkins goes out of his way to avoid me?" Sara dropped sugar cubes in her teacup.

"No," Patricia replied as she poured tea. "It's probably your imagination."

"I'm certain of it."

"Well, if it is true, you should be grateful. You're

better off not drawing his attention. He's quite a notorious heartbreaker.''

Something about Patricia's expression gave Sara cause to wonder if her friend had been speaking from experience. Shoving the thought aside, Sara decided Patricia had given her sound advice. In truth, Brody owed her nothing, neither a nod nor a smile.

Chapter Six

The sunlight quickly fading, Brody stood observing the scene on the street below. Donald Gilbert had just closed the door behind Sara and was now helping her into his awaiting coach. Word was going around that Curtis Farmington and Donald had become her favorite escorts. Brody had to give Patricia credit. She had turned Sara into a graceful swan.

As the coach pulled away, Brody took a long drag on his cigar then let the smoke trail slowly from his lips. There were going to be some mighty disappointed young bucks before long. Though Sara had become a swan, she was still high-spirited, and none of her suitors were experienced enough to handle her. Before they realized it she'd be walking all over them and they wouldn't have a thing to show for their efforts. No promise of wedlock and no bedroom privileges. He suspected that the only man she'd consider bedding would be older and one who would bring business to her company. However, if she had the same effect on them as she'd had on others, the young bucks would still be enamoured.

Brody dropped the half-smoked cigar into the cuspidor then shoved his hands deep into his trouser pockets. He'd been tempted to warn Harriet Gilbert that her grandson was in danger of ending up with a broken heart, but he doubted that any of the Baronesses would care to hear his theories.

Sara had the Baronesses convinced that she was the nicest, sweetest person to have graced the entire territory of Kansas in years. If anyone dared spout a wrong word about Sara, the women labeled it jealousy. And from all indications, Sara made sure that impression remained intact. She knew exactly how much power those four women wielded. As it turned out, it was the relationship between the five that had made him decide to avoid the charming Miss Miles.

Brody turned from the window, sat behind his desk and stretched his long legs. There were few times when the big building was almost empty, leaving him alone with his thoughts. This had turned out to be just one of those nights, and he welcomed it. Enough thinking about Sara Miles. There were far more pleasant things to contemplate, like Otis Wooten's challenge this afternoon that his horse could beat anything in Brody's stable.

Brody closed his eyes, relaxed and entertained himself with thoughts of the upcoming horse race. For the past two months, Otis had bragged to everyone about the new stallion he'd brought from England. Brody had known all along that it was only a matter of time before the rotund man challenged him to a race. The race had been set for Sunday.

Brody chuckled. No one knew about the two-year-old horse bred and raised on his ranch twenty miles out of town. The bay was faster than his famous sire and Brody had been waiting for just such an opportunity to present him. He not only believed Runaway couldn't be beaten, he was willing to back it with a considerable amount of money.

"Coming to the race was a wonderful idea," Sara stated as Colonel Jack Singleton helped her from the buggy. "I didn't expect so many people."

Though Sara seldom went out with Jack, when she did she always felt comfortable. He was like an old pair of slippers one didn't want to throw away.

"I thought you'd enjoy the occasion. There hasn't been a race of this magnitude for several years. Last time, Brody's horse left Otis's horse in the dust. Otis is eager to get even."

Jack offered Sara the crook of his elbow and Sara gladly slipped her arm beneath it. Due to the multitude of people, Jack had to leave the buggy a distance from the big home on the hill, and the ground was rough beneath Sara's feet.

"I doubt that there's a horse in Kansas or Missouri

that could beat Brody's stable. That's why Otis went to England to purchase Ebon's Victory.''

''He went all the way to England just to get a horse that could beat Mr. Hawkins's steed? That seems unbelievable. It must have cost a fortune.'' She stepped over a clot of dirt. So many people and horses moving about were digging up the ground.

''Money means nothing to these men, Sara.'' He chuckled. ''They have to spend it on something. I wish I could say the same.''

Sara agreed.

As they joined the crowd of people milling about, Sara could feel the excitement in the air. This was so much bigger than the occasional races she'd seen back home.

Food and drink had been laid out, but Jack and the other spectators were more interested in the horses tethered about. To Sara, all the entries were magnificent-looking animals. Better than anything she was used to seeing, which made her wonder why Otis and Brody's mounts would be considered superior stock.

''There'll probably be a couple of races before the big one,'' Jack informed Sara as he slid a knowing hand down the flank of a chestnut entry.

The red-faced man standing next to Jack grinned, showing stained teeth. ''I figured you'd be here, Colonel.'' He spat tobacco juice onto the ground.

"Greetings, Mr. Smith," Jack acknowledged. "Nothing could have kept me away."

"I felt the same. Have you heard the news?"

"What news?"

"Otis and Hawkins's horses are racing alone."

"You don't say?" Jack uttered in obvious surprise.

"The owners got together and decided they had nothing to gain by racing against those two, so they're having their own race. Frankly, I don't blame them. Have you seen Runaway and Ebon's Victory?"

"No."

"They're down there in their paddocks. In them stables."

After introductions were made, the men resumed their conversation. Curious, Sara strolled in the direction Mr. Smith had pointed. She nodded, smiled and said a few words to people she knew, but never broke stride. For some reason she wasn't in the mood for chitchat.

Seeing a cluster of people at the front of the brick stable, Sara decided to enter by the back. As she rounded the corner, she came within an inch of slamming into Brody Hawkins's broad chest. Only some fast footwork kept a disaster from occurring. Without uttering a word, she continued on. She didn't dare look back. She knew a pair of sea-green eyes were watching every step she took.

"Just follow my instructions and you won't have

any trouble,'' Sara heard Brody say to the short man he'd been talking to before her interruption.

A soft nicker caught Sara's attention. She looked into one of the stalls. The Shetland pony standing at the far end of the stall tossed its head. Undoubtedly it belonged to one of Otis's children. She was about to continue on when she felt the presence of someone behind her.

''Be careful, the pony bites.''

Sara would have recognized that deep voice anywhere. She turned her back to him and glanced round at the other stalls. ''You couldn't possibly be speaking to me, could you?''

''What?'' Brody asked, confused by the question.

Finally he realized what the bright-eyed woman had been alluding to.

Sara turned and looked the culprit in the eye. She placed her hand on her chest and feigned surprise. ''Oh, Mr. Hawkins! You really *are* talking to me. Please, forgive me. I'm so honored.'' She sneered and moved to the next stall.

Brody slowly trailed after her. ''You've noticed my lack of attention.''

Sara could hear humor in his voice. ''How could I not? As a matter of fact, it was pointed out to me by the Baronesses.'' A lie, but it sounded good.

''And what were the ladies' comments on the matter?''

Sara looked into another stall. Brody was standing

too close and she could smell the rich combination of fresh tossed hay, earth and sun that seemed to be emanating from him. "Patricia said I should feel blessed."

"Patricia?" His sudden laughter spooked the nearby horses. "You spoke to Patricia about it?"

Realizing the stall she'd been staring into was empty, Sara quickly moved to the next one. "Well, no...not exactly." She hadn't meant to mention Patricia's name. "She was there when the Baronesses were pointing it out to me." Another lie.

"I see. Well, pray tell, what was their consensus?"

Sara forced herself to face him again. She had to grab hold of the half door. The devilish grin on the man's handsome face made her knees weak. "They said it's obvious to them that you're attracted to me but you don't want to admit it." Sara had to fight to keep from laughing. The stunned look on his face was priceless.

"Since we are momentarily alone," she continued, "perhaps you'll explain why I've been deliberately snubbed. It's not as if we haven't spoken before. And even if that were the case I have serious doubts that that would have stopped you."

Brody cocked a dark brow. "Apparently my lack of attention has caused considerable thought."

"Please don't insult me by trying to make something of this that isn't. It's the misuse of etiquette that bothers me and the fact that others have taken notice."

A horse nudged her shoulder causing her to jump. "It's a matter of civility," she blurted out.

Lips pursed, Brody studied the petite woman caressing the horse's muzzle. "Perhaps it bothers you that I'm not kowtowing like the other bachelors who seem to thrive on your every word?"

"You can hardly cast stones. You don't seem to lack female attention."

"Sara! I wondered where you had gone," Jack called as he approached.

Brody cocked his head at seeing who Sara's escort was. "A perfect example of what I was just talking about," he whispered.

"Perhaps it bothers *you* that men find me attractive," she snapped back at him.

"Not at all."

When Jack joined them, the two men shook hands.

"I've been looking at the stallions," Jack commented, "and I still can't decide which one to place my wager on."

"That's quite a compliment coming from someone who knows horses as well as you. Needless to say, I'm hoping I'll be the winner. I don't want to have to listen to Otis's bragging for the rest of my life." Brody turned to Sara. "It was nice talking to you, Miss Miles. We'll have to resume our conversation at another time." He tipped his hat. "Thank you for wishing me luck."

"Did I interrupt something?" Jack asked when Brody was out of hearing distance.

"Not at all. Where is his horse?"

"This way."

Sara followed.

"It was nice of you to wish him luck."

"I didn't." Sara offered no further explanation.

Never, in all her years, could Sara remember seeing so magnificent an animal as the one in the stall before her. Like his master, Runaway was tall and powerful. Sara felt such warmth when the big stallion turned and looked at her. "Can you place a wager for me? Strictly in confidence."

Jack nodded. "But you haven't seen Otis's mount."

"I don't have to. This horse isn't going to let anyone beat him." Sara pulled money from her purse and handed it to him.

"No, no," Jack insisted. "Let me take care of the wager."

Sara smiled. "I don't want to share my winnings with you, and I don't want to feel obligated."

"Sara, what did Brody mean when he said something about resuming your conversation?"

"It meant nothing."

"Good. As a friend I would advise you to stay away from him."

Sara patted his callused hand. "I know you only speak from concern, Jack, but I'm quite capable of taking care of myself."

"I'll go place your wager."

Sara knew Jack would have preferred a closer relationship, but he was wise enough to know there would never be anything between them except friendship.

The stallion snorted and pawed at the fresh hay in his stall. Sara backed away just before the beast surged forward, stopping just before hitting the gate. Sara shook her head at him. "Shame on you. That's no way to treat a lady."

Runaway flicked his ears forward.

Sara laughed. "You just enjoy scaring people. Well, it's not going to work with me." She stepped forward.

The bay snorted and tossed his head.

"Cut that out. If you're a good boy and behave yourself, I'll rub your nose."

Runaway moved his head to within her reach.

Hearing a deep chuckle, Sara turned. Brody Hawkins stood behind her holding a saddle.

"He likes you."

"I thought you had left."

"I came to get my horse."

Instead of a sharp retort, Sara walked away. Mr. Hawkins's sudden friendliness did nothing but make her angrier. How gracious of him to finally allow her an audience!

People were lined up along the graded track, talking anxiously, eager to see the race between the two magnificent horses. All day money had exchanged hands and now the moment of truth was upon them. Brody and Otis had given their young jockeys their instructions; now like the others, the two men could only stand and watch.

The mounts were at the starting line, both dancing sideways, tossing their heads and pushing at the bits, but the riders kept a tight hold on the reins.

A shot.

Brody watched the horses leap forward, Runaway ahead by a breath. Dirt flew into the air as they gained speed, their mighty hooves pounding the ground. Neck to neck they ate up the distance. Muscles bulged. Sleek bodies glistening in the sunlight. A hush fell over everyone as they watched in awe at perfection in motion.

Catching a movement out of the corner of his eyes, Brody glanced across the track. He couldn't help but be amused by Sara's show of excitement. Instead of cheering, she tossed her parasol back and forth and Jack had to keep dodging it. He suddenly became fascinated by the look on her face. Sara Miles had indeed come alive.

Brody returned his attention to the race, but found himself repeatedly taking peeks and having second thoughts about the beauty he'd chosen to avoid.

The moment Brody saw his horse win by barely a nose, he again looked at Sara. By her enthusiasm, he knew she had placed a wager on Runaway, which for some reason pleased him.

Still jubilant, Sara reached up and kissed Jack on the cheek. "What is she doing with a man old enough to be her father?" Brody muttered. Probably making sure the fort contracts didn't slip from her fingers.

Brody lost sight of Sara when people gathered around him, patting him on the back and offering praises to Runaway. He finally managed to pull himself free from the congratulators and went looking for Otis.

Though deeply disappointed, Otis took his loss well and ended up enjoying his own party. Even after a huge supper had been provided for his guests, the main topic of conversation was still the race. Some were insisting that it proved nothing. The best horse could only be determined by two out of three wins.

"Thank you for taking me," Sara said as Jack drove her home. "I had a wonderful time. Have you decided to accept the transfer to Washington?"

Jack nodded.

"I shall hate seeing you go, even if it is a big promotion. You've been a good friend. I hope I get along as well with the new commander as I have with you."

"I've made sure your contracts are good for another three years, my dear. By then, you'll be well established."

Chapter Seven

Sara was certain she had reached the apex of expectancy when the time came to take the wagons out of storage. Lucas would see that they were thoroughly checked and any necessary repairs made. He had already started negotiating the purchase of any needed stock. With March creeping up, the 325-mile stretch from Independence to Council Bluffs was already swarming with teamsters arriving from the East.

For the first time, her wagons, each loaded with approximately seven thousands pounds of goods, would go out on the trail with some 780 other wagons. How could she not be excited?

But even with all that was going on in her life, Sara still made it a point to have tea with the Baronesses once a week. The only other social functions she attended were those that she knew for certain Mr. Hawkins would also attend.

She had still not forgiven him for his rude treatment.

So, she had decided to repay the man for his insults in the only manner she knew how. She'd chosen to extend to him the same courtesy he'd given her. She made a deliberate and very obvious point of ignoring him.

At Lester Gilbert's party she'd grabbed her escort's arm and had insisted they leave. She'd caught sight of Hawkins headed in her direction. Just before leaving the room, she'd turned to take one last look at the mighty Brody Hawkins. For a change, the expression on his face made it quite clear that he knew exactly what she was up to.

Satisfaction kept Sara on a cloud for an entire week. Unfortunately, everything seemed to go downhill after that. Retribution was not really her cup of tea. And she had become uncomfortable at the way he kept his distance but continually watched her. He reminded her of a predator waiting for just the right moment to strike.

With all the preparations, meetings with financial backers and firms, contracts and all else, time moved swiftly. By early April, Sara was still bogged down with work. But one afternoon, she couldn't resist stopping her buggy and watching a riverboat coming into dock, its deep horn blasts bringing townspeople flocking. The sight still sent adrenaline pumping through her body.

The moment the boat docked, the crew quickly

thrust planks out onto the dock and the stevedores swarmed aboard. Within minutes the first of them came back down the gangplanks, carrying the cargo to one of many warehouses.

Sara flicked the reins across the horse's shiny rump, slowly moving the buggy forward. As she tried to thread her way toward the office, she barely managed to contain her excitement upon seeing the streets blockaded with hundreds of freight wagons, thousands of oxen and mules, cattle, bales, boxes and everything else that would be headed west.

Her wagons had been some of the first to move out onto the eight-hundred-mile stretch to Sante Fe. The third outfit would leave tonight.

With all the obstacles blocking the streets, Sara decided to make a wide detour then reigned the horse toward home. The afternoon was growing late and she could take her time getting ready for Patricia's ball tonight.

Chapter Eight

Sara wondered what she was doing there at the ball.

Half listening to the music and the Baronesses gossiping about different guests arriving at Patricia's show of opulence, Sara had suddenly realized that the excitement of being a social butterfly had lost its appeal. Patricia had taken the time to polish a rough stone by showing her how to dress and act. But what then?

With servants, nannies and so forth, the women of position had nothing to do but throw lavish soirees and spend their husbands' money. Sara had discovered another truth that had left her unsettled. It had taken awhile for her to open her eyes and see that Patricia was attracted to other men. It had also become painfully obvious that Brody Hawkins was one of them.

Sara winced upon seeing Curtis Farmington coming toward her. She had grown tired of the men who squired her about.

Curtis made a slight bow. "May I have this dance?"

"Thank you, Curtis, but I'm not really feeling well." She placed a hand on her stomach to emphasis her plight. "Perhaps later." She was grateful he left peacefully instead of trying to change her mind.

"You're not feeling well?"

Sara looked down at Nallie Wooten. "Truly, I'm feeling fine. I just don't care to dance right now."

"You don't seem to be enjoying yourself, my dear," Clara added. She reached over and patted Sara's arm.

The ladies continued their gossiping.

Sara dabbed her nose with her lace handkerchief for lack of anything else to do. Clara is right, she thought. She wasn't enjoying herself. She'd be far more content to talk to Lucas or any of the men who worked for her. She enjoyed listening to their tales, but they were all gone now.

Strange, after being thrown into a life full of parties, she finally understood why her father had stayed at the same location and had kept the same friends instead of building a nice big house on the outskirts of town.

Sara leaned down and tapped Clara's shoulder. "I'm going home."

"But you only arrived less than an hour ago."

"I have so much work to do tomorrow and I'd like to get a good night's rest."

"Are you sure you're not coming down with something? Maybe I should have a mustard plaster fixed and sent to your house.''

"No, I'll be fine. I'll see you in a couple of days."

Sara headed for the doorway just as Brody entered the ballroom. Immediately she turned away, looking for another exit. Left with no recourse, she walked out into the garden and waited.

After a good five minutes, and convinced she could leave without having to confront her nemesis, Sara took a step forward, then paused. The French doors were open and she had no problem seeing most of the guests. Where had his lordship gone?

Suddenly Sara was jerked around and shoved against the wall of the house, the shadows swallowing her. A quick flash of candlelight from inside gave her a glimpse of Brody Hawkins's stern face.

"What are you doing?" Sara demanded.

"I'm warning you that I'm not someone you want to play games with, darling. Nor am I one of your puppets that you offer promises to without fulfillment. Beware of what you start with me, Sara. You may discover you've bitten off more than you can chew."

"I don't know what you're talking about."

"I'm talking about your obvious avoidance."

"I see. It's all right if you do it but it's different if I do it?" She tried to push him away, but his hard, muscled body was pressed against hers, making the effort useless. "Turn me loose," she said with as much bravado as she could muster.

"The word is *please*."

Sara remained silent.

Brody cupped the back of her neck with his hand. She tried pushing against it. But his hand was like a vice. Slowly, deliberately he forced her head forward until their lips were barely touching.

"Please," he insisted.

Everything seemed to come to a standstill at the taste of his warm breath and his lips brushing against hers. But somehow Sara managed to remained firm. "I'll not say please to a man who thinks he can get by with rudeness."

Sara thought they couldn't be any closer until the arm circling her waist tightened, pulling her against him, molding her body to his. His body heat became hers, as did the air he breathed.

"Please," he repeated softly, as his tongue traced the contour of her lips.

Sara's body had turned into a limp rag, her throat seemed to have lost all moisture and words were difficult to come by. He was deliberately torturing her. Even her nipples had become firm from his hard chest pressing against them.

"Maybe I misunderstood." He continued his assault by trailing his tongue down her neck then kissed the swell of her breast. "Perhaps you don't want me to turn you loose."

Desperate, Sara gushed out, "Please!"

"Now that wasn't so hard, was it?"

A fresh, cool breeze brushed across her face, bringing her back to reality. ''You are the lowest form of man. You're lower than the lowest rat! You've no integrity. Now let me go.''

''Be careful, my sweet. The more you antagonize me the more appealing you become.''

Sara was about to offer a snide retort when his lips captured hers. At first she struggled, but his kiss was not meant to be a quick peck. His tongue coaxed her lips apart, allowing him deep inside. He sapped away any fight left in her as the kiss deepened, demanding, ravaging and stealing away her very soul. He stoked a flame that quickly turned into an inferno. An inferno that left her willing to be burned.

She felt wicked.

She felt alive.

Never had she been so thoroughly kissed, and when his lips parted from hers, she wanted more.

It was the cool dampness of the bricks against her back that slowly brought Sara back to earth. She was alone, but her lips still burned. The thought of him so easily igniting such passion both excited and frightened her. How could she have been so susceptible to such a rogue?

Sara forced herself to stand on both feet while straightening her shoulders. How could she have ever thought that all kisses were the same?

Before returning to the ballroom, she checked to be

sure her gown still hung in an orderly fashion. Could anyone tell what had just happened?

Sara headed straight for the door, grabbed her wrap and left. She couldn't bear the thought of anyone seeing how flushed her cheeks were.

During the following month, Sara sent notes of apology to any invitations received, with the excuse that she had too much work to do. A reply that few wealthy women seemed to understand. It wasn't exactly a lie. She had already hired two more clerks and had purchased the entire building to house her growing company.

Being bored with the social life had been one of her reasons for staying away, and though she hated to admit it, Brody had scared her. She didn't know what to do about him. He had been right. She was out of her league when it came to dealing with him.

If he could cause such an emotional reaction with one kiss, what else was he capable of doing to her? But oh, what a glorious kiss it had been. Just thinking about it turned her to honey. Had he enjoyed the kiss as much as she had?

After reviewing the situation, Sara deduced that she had nothing to worry about. She was no longer interested in shunning Mr. Hawkins. She'd accomplished what she'd set out to do and as long as she stopped deliberately avoiding him, he'd leave her alone. Or so he had indicated before stealing a kiss.

* * *

Sara stood precariously on a ladder placing the old ledgers Peter handed her onto new shelves when Brody unexpectedly stepped into her office. Startled, the ledgers slipped from her arms, and she would have followed them to the floor had she not caught her balance in time.

"Leave us alone," Brody said to the young clerk.

"Don't you leave this room!" Sara ordered.

That wasn't what Peter wanted to hear. He looked at his employer climbing down the ladder, then at the intruder. Brody Hawkins had to be a foot taller and twice his size. Faithful to his employer, Peter remained glued to the floor, but he was praying awfully hard that the stranger wouldn't do him any physical harm.

Without further ado, Brody picked the skinny runt up by the collar and the seat of his pants and shoved him out the door. He gave the other employees a stern look before closing the door and turning the large key.

"Now that we're alone—" he turned, his gaze resting on the cocked pistol Sara had pointing at his chest. "My, my, what have we here? I hope you know how to use it. I certainly don't care to have a wild bullet between my eyes."

"I've worked around men too long to not have a gun handy. How dare you come here and order my people about? If you need to bark orders do it in your own building! Now unlock that door and get out."

"Damned if this doesn't beat all." Placing his

Sara and the Rogue

hands on his hips, he stared at the woman confronting him. "In the first place, I didn't bark orders. I came here to discuss something. Is it just me or do you treat everyone like this?"

Perhaps Sara had been a bit hasty about grabbing the pistol, but she couldn't back down now. "You usurped my authority. How am I supposed to know what crazy things you might try to do?"

"So you draw a gun on me?" he asked in disbelief. His eyes locked with hers. "Lady, do you seriously think that gun could prevent me from doing something I'd set my mind to?"

A shiver of warning ran up Sara's spine.

"I came for a reason and I'm not leaving until I've had my say."

His deep voice wasn't raised, but he seemed all the more threatening because of it. "Then have your say and be done with it." He took a step forward, but Sara held her ground. "Don't make the mistake of thinking I won't shoot."

"You haven't been to any of the socials lately. Why?"

To Sara's dismay, he moved toward the bookshelves instead of the closed door. "Why is it that every time we meet, you're giving orders or insisting I answer questions? You don't own me. You don't even know me."

"Nor you me, or you wouldn't be so sure you presently have the upper hand. At least do me the favor of answering my question." He took another step forward. "Why haven't you been attending any social functions?"

"Not that it's any of your business, but I have work to do. I'll remind you it's how I make my living. I've answered your question, now go."

"It had nothing to do with me?"

"You flatter yourself."

"You have people wondering why you chose to blatantly ignore me and now rumors are floating around that I made unwanted advances."

"You did."

"Lessons learned."

He took another step and Sara pulled the trigger.

A rush of footsteps could be heard on the other side of the door.

"Are you all right, Miss Miles?" a clerk called upon finding the door locked.

"Yes," Sara answered as she stared in disbelief at the bullet hole less than an inch from the toe of Brody's boot. Pulling the trigger had unnerved her more than it had him. Fear was to blame. Fear of his touch...of losing control. Look how foolishly she had reacted to being alone in a closed room with him.

Sara squared her shoulders. "Get out or the next shot will be in your leg," she bluffed.

"Rumor now is that you're staying away for fear of what I might do."

"Do?" How could he act so blasé after what she

had just done? Never, in her entire life, had she done anything quite so foolish.

There were a lot of things Brody could tolerate from others, but having someone shoot at him wasn't one of them. He looked unexpectedly toward the door. Sara did the same. Making her look away gave him the opportunity he'd waited for. He lunged forward. Catching her off guard, he had no problem snatching the pistol from her hand and tossing it onto the desk.

"Now what are you going to do, my dear?"

Sara made a dash for the door, but the room was too small. He stepped to the side, blocking any escape. Sara backed away with him following like a big cat ready to pounce.

"Don't you think that if I'm to be accused of something I might as well enjoy it?"

"Yes…I mean no…I—" She was trapped against the wall and he had just closed the little distance between them.

"Why did you think you needed a weapon?"

"You were physical with my clerk and you want to close me down." The words barely made it past her throat.

"Close you down? If that had been my purpose it would have already been done."

He stood too close for comfort. "Who knows what you might do?" she said.

"And what do you think might have been on my mind? Another kiss? Why would that frighten you?"

He slowly traced the outline of her lips with his finger. "Or were you afraid what the kiss might lead to? Did you create the latest gossip so I would return?"

"That's ridiculous," Sara stated, her breathing labored. "Contrary to what your conceit is telling you, any slights on my part have had nothing to do with you. I have been too tired at night to go anywhere. But if it will satisfy your pride, I'll make occasional appearances at friends' soirees."

"It's too late." He looked down at her partially opened lips. The bottom lip twitched, as if inviting him to taste the hidden pleasures. He trailed his finger down her neck, stopping at the curve and feeling the rhythm of her heartbeat. Her intake of breath caused her breasts to rub softly against him. "It's going to happen."

It wasn't fair that she had to resist him while fighting her own desires. "What's going to happen?" Sara's determination was melting faster than butter on a hot roll and her heart was pounding double time against her ribs. Not from fear, but God help her, from anticipation.

His kiss was so light she barely felt it.

"You'll eventually be in my bed, exactly where I want you."

Sara gasped at his boldness. "It will never happen," she growled.

"Oh, but it will. I can guarantee it."

They were both startled when the door suddenly crashed in and a giant of a man entered the room.

Seeing the fury on her wagon master's face, Sara quickly said, "I'm all right, Lucas."

To Sara's horror, as Brody moved away, his mouth curved into a slight smile. Surely he wasn't considering a fight with Lucas? That would be pure suicide.

"The gossip I spoke to you about is going to have to be resolved, one way or another," Brody said as he moved to the doorway.

"You, sir, are a ruthless cad," Sara bravely accused, knowing she was safe. But Brody's half-cocked smile made her back away.

"Sara, my dear, you haven't even an inkling as to how ruthless I can be if I really want something."

When he'd left, Sara released the air from her lungs. Had he just made a threat? She collapsed onto a chair and viewed the broken door. She should make him pay for it.

Sara looked at Lucas, his expression still showing concern. "Thank you for coming to my rescue, but I really wasn't in any danger."

"You're all right?"

"Yes, I'm fine. Mr. Hawkins was spouting a bunch of useless verbal threats, nothing more." She could see Lucas relax.

"For a moment, I thought I was about to have a fight on my hands."

"I doubt it. I believe Mr. Hawkins has enough sense not to do something as foolish as that."

Lucas shook his head. "I don't know. You didn't see the look in his eyes when I came barging in."

When everyone had returned to work, Sara went over in her mind what had just taken place. She'd be wise to tread lightly at doing anything that might involve Brody Hawkins. The man was absolutely dangerous. However, she had accomplished something. He'd never try snubbing her again.

No doubt about it, Brody thought as he dodged a fast-moving wagon before making it to the other side of the street. The gossip is really going to heat up now. Especially after Sara's employees had heard the gunshot. It had left unanswered questions, and had given free rein to imaginations that would blow everything out of proportion.

He entered his building. It would probably end up with men snickering and saying he'd almost been caught with his pants down. Or that he'd been in the midst of forcing himself on poor defenseless Sara Miles when her wagon master barged in and put an end to it. Or possibly there'd even be a tale about how he'd fought to get away while the wagon master defended Sara's honor.

He took the stairs two at a time.

Oh, yes, Brody thought, the men who knew him would be laughing and applauding from here to Europe. On the other hand, the women would pretend to be aghast while at the same time dying of curiosity as to why he'd felt the need to do such a thing when he could have any woman he wanted.

Actually he wouldn't give a damn as to what anyone said if it had been with anyone besides the Baronesses' so-called adopted daughter.

Brody walked into his office and headed straight to the mahogany liquor cabinet. He downed a shot of whiskey, then poured another before moving to his favorite place to think.

The window.

As on other occasions, he noted that the sky had very little color. It never seemed as blue in town as it did on the prairie. At unexpected times like these, Brody felt a longing to return to the past and his old self. Had this afternoon been in the old days, the entire episode with Sara would have had an entirely different ending. Not too many years ago he would have taken care of her wagon master, chased the employees out, shoved everything off the desk and taken Sara then and there.

The idea still had tremendous appeal. But this wasn't the past, and if he did have a choice between then and now, he'd choose now. He'd built an empire and no one had the nerve or the ability to usurp his power...until a shrimp of a woman who had more guts than most men had decided to get even for being ignored.

He shook his head and finished his drink. He walked over and set the empty glass on top of the liquor cabinet. To this day he could still recall the ache in his belly while waiting for his mother to dole out his meager ration of food, and the feel of patched holes in the soles of his hand-me-down shoes.

Twelve children had been born to his parents, poor tenant farmers. He had been the ninth. Like the others before him, he'd left home so there would be fewer mouths to feed.

He could remember working his way across country from farm to farm for food and a place to lay his head for the night. He hadn't known how to read or write and his chances of survival had been questionable.

Brody flopped down on the leather sofa allowing the memories to come flooding back.

As always happened when he slipped back in time, there were the mental pictures of Amy Baker that had turned hazy over the years.

He had been around fourteen when he'd reached the Widow Baker's farm. A smile softened his lips.

Amy Baker had lost her husband and two sons to the pox. When he'd gone to work for her she'd treated him like a son.

Night after night she'd worked to teach him numbers and to read and write so he could have a future. With her encouragement and several dozen books that had been her husband's, Brody spent every spare minute reading.

More than once, Amy had said she wanted to make sure that when he left, he could hold his head high among men and become anything he wanted to. Naturally he'd sworn he would never go away.

Amy had different plans. When she'd sent him away, it was with a horse and saddle, money in his pack and a promise to not look back. He'd never seen her again.

He looked toward the window. Did time ever really change a man? He didn't think so. It just taught him how to hide his faults. He'd worked hard to get where he was. His house and social standing were all part of a long-range plan set into motion many years ago. Within the next two years he'd add the finishing touches. He'd marry some socialite from the East who would provide him status and sons.

Leavenworth had become a large cultured and sophisticated town. Unspoken social boundaries had already slipped into place. Boundaries that dictated what constituted the elite. The Baronesses had unconsciously started it, but other ladies from wealthy families had moved to Leavenworth, bringing stricter standards.

But it was still those same four women who, with a flick of their finger, could ruin his plans. Therein lay his problem. After what had happened in Sara's office, the ladies were bound to hear about it. They would ask Sara for a report, she'd say he threatened her, and his political plans would come to an early end.

He had been very diligent at winning the Baronesses' favor. He'd flattered, at times flirted, made sure his manners were flawless and built a home that was the envy of everyone. All aimed at becoming the governor of the future state of Kansas. He didn't even want to contemplate what his chances would be if Miss Miles's influence turned the Baronesses against him. Which she would likely do after what had happened at her office.

Sara Miles's independence and determination reminded him of Amy. And like Amy he had to give Sara her due. She'd created a company practically out of nothing. And not just by taking work from others. She had managed to drum up her own business as well, a feat many others had failed to do. But when it came to trickery, he could beat her around every corner.

The time had come to take matters into his own hands—before Sara Miles could destroy his future.

Strange how things worked out. He'd stayed away from the wildcat to avoid trouble. Now he needed her to help quiet rumors that made him look the villain.

Once that had been accomplished, he'd bed her. The ache in his groin had started when he'd observed her at the race. He would have her and she'd come willingly. It was just a matter of time and deliberate planning.

Chapter Nine

Sara reread the note:

"Miss Miles, Please accept my apology for my ungentlemanly conduct yesterday, and allow me to make amends. I would consider it an honor if you'd permit me to escort you to the annual summer ball. B.H."

Sara finished her breakfast, then read the note again. She wanted to go to the ball. Just the thought of Brody's arm circling her waist as he glided her around the dance floor made her pulse beat overtime. And everyone would see that Mr. Hawkins found her just as appealing as the other women he escorted about. As her father had been fond of saying, the time had come to look the truth in the eye.

From her first meeting with Brody, she had been torn between unbelievable desire and total dislike for the man. Two emotions that didn't blend. Hadn't she been told more than once that the broken hearts he'd left behind were numerous? The time had come to listen to warnings and look to the future. With Brody, there was no future.

She wouldn't forgo her integrity and stand in the man's shadow as other women had done. And she most certainly would not ruin her reputation by allowing herself to be counted as one of his conquests.

The following morning, Brody tossed the handwritten note onto the bed then stood still while the tailor completed the adjustments on his new evening clothes.

"Will there be a reply, sir?" his valet inquired, the small silver tray that had held the message still clasped in his hand.

"No reply. Have Bobby Ray saddle General and bring him around to the front of the house. Is this going to take much longer?" he asked the tailor.

The valet silently left the room.

"Only a minute more, Mr. Hawkins."

"Good. I have matters to attend to."

Ten minutes later, Brody left the house.

"Another nice day, eh, Mr. Hawkins?" the stable boy asked as Brody mounted the gelding the boy held by the bit.

Brody's reply was a gruff grunt. He took the reins and touched his heels to the horse's sides. The spirited animal pranced around, his neck bowed as he tried to oust the bit with his tongue, but Brody had no problem getting General under control. A moment later he had the gray trotting down the circular drive and away from the house, his long tail swishing from side to side.

As far as Brody was concerned, the only way the day could look brighter would be for Nallie Wooten to believe he had been unjustly criticized about Sara. Pushing seventy-one, she was the youngest of Baronesses. She had always said she had a soft heart when it came to romance. She definitely had a twinkle in her eye whenever she looked at him. That twinkle was what he was relying on.

Since Sara had confessed to him that the Baronesses thought Brody ignored her because he was attracted, he'd let them think they had been right all along. Like it or not, Sara would accompany him to the ball.

That afternoon Nallie called the Baronesses to her house for a meeting.

Two days later Sara joined the ladies at Harriet Gilbert's home for what had become their weekly tea.

After a half hour of discussions on subjects such as the garden Sara wanted to start at her house, plus mutual friends and weather, Clara brought up the subject on everyone's mind, except Sara's.

"You're still planning to come to our ball, aren't you, Sara?" Bertha asked.

"We'd be terribly disappointed if you didn't."

Nallie's raspy voice always made Sara think of a carrot being grated. "Of course I am."

"We know how busy you've been," Bertha added.

Sara placed her teacup on the saucer and smiled. "I wouldn't miss it for anything." She took another one of the sugar cookies with dabs of blackberry jam on top. "Nallie, these are delicious."

"An old recipe. If you'd get a cook as we've suggested, I'd make sure she had the recipe."

"I hired one two days ago. She's wonderful. Patricia found her for me. Patricia also has a housekeeper who she said is very efficient and is willing to start next week."

Harriet clapped her hands. "Maybe now you'll put some meat on your bones."

"Before long I'll be as big as a sow and I'll never fit into the new gown I'm having made especially for your grand ball.

"Who is to be your escort?" Bertha asked nonchalantly. Seeing that her cup was empty, and Harriet was making no effort to play hostess, she poured her own drink, adding just a smidgen of Clara's Kentucky whiskey.

Sara thought a minute as she dabbed her lips with the delicate linen napkin. "I'm ashamed to say I haven't given it much thought. I've had several offers, but none interest me." She laughed softly. "Not nearly as many as I've had on other occasions. I do believe the local bachelors are giving up on me."

"You've turned down invitations to the ball?"

Sara looked at them. "Yes, I have."

A strange look passed between the others.

"Is something wrong?" Sara asked suspiciously. She took another bite of the cookie.

"You told Brody Hawkins you had already made arrangements for the evening."

Sara choked on a cookie crumb. Brody had discussed his offer with them? "Telling him I had already made other arrangements seemed the appropriate response at the time. It was nicer than saying what was really on my mind. Did he speak to you about our last confrontation?"

"Yes, he did," Nallie said sadly. "And of course there is some gossip floating around. Needless to say it is quite different than his version of the story." Nallie sighed. "I felt so sorry for him."

"Why?" Sara asked with raised eyebrows. Her hackles were rising. She had a strong feeling that she wasn't going to like what was about to be said. Especially if it had to do with Mr. Hawkins.

"Brody told me the other morning that to his own surprise, he has become quite smitten with you."

Sara could hardly believe what she was hearing. This had to do with her refusal to accompany him. Lord in heaven, the man would stop at nothing to get what he wanted!

"He's not telling the truth!" She rose from the sofa. "I won't hear any more."

"Oh, please don't leave," Nallie whined.

Sara immediately felt guilty. How could she act so

intolerant to these very women who had been so good to her?

"I'm sorry," Sara apologized. "Just the mention of that man gets me riled."

"Come sit back down." Clara patted the seat beside her. "We believe we have this situation between you and Brody all figured out."

Dreading to hear the conclusion that had apparently been reached, Sara resumed her seat on the horsehair sofa, her back ramrod straight.

By the time Sara turned her buggy homeward, her head was swimming and her temples were pounding. According to what she had been told, Brody Hawkins confided to Nallie that he had suddenly found himself attracted to Sara. However, due to misunderstandings between them, he hadn't yet had an opportunity to find out if something could develop between them.

He had actually told Nallie, and she'd quoted all dreamy-eyed, "If I could prove to her that I'm not the ogre she believes me to be, we might come to like each other...and who knows where that could lead? But she refuses to be seen with me. I asked to escort her to your ball. She said she had already made other arrangements."

Sara loosened her hold on the reins. She had been grasping them so tightly her fingers had become numb.

So Brody Hawkins had won their battle of wills, Sara thought bitterly. After trying to get the Baronesses to believe he'd told nothing but lies, she'd finally had no choice but to give in and agree with them.

"But what if he spoke the truth?" Nallie had asked.

Hattie smiled. "And why not make peace with him? It would do more good than harm."

"What harm could there be in accompanying him to the ball?" Clara sipped her tea. "Others would see that he isn't making unwanted advances."

That last statement made Sara realize why Mr. Hawkins was so determined to take her to the ball. Gossip! He had said so in her office. He had always struck her as a man who would laugh off such things. Why was gossip so important to him?

Sara drove the small buggy into the carriage house. Tim, lying on a bale of straw, woke immediately.

"Did you have a big meal?" Sara climbed down from the buggy.

He rubbed his stomach and smiled. "Yes, ma'am. Cook's got your supper waitin'."

Her first day in town, Sara had found the ten-year-old boy begging for food. She'd kept him with her until she could put him in charge of the carriage house. He had proven more than thankful and a hard worker.

As Sara walked toward the back entrance of the house, the lights coming from inside gave her a warm feeling. She stopped a moment and looked up at the harvest moon. Clouds were starting to form but they didn't look as if they were carrying rain.

She continued down the path, feeling especially vulnerable. She had lost her first battle with Brody when she had finally agreed to accompany him to the ball in order to keep peace with the Baronesses.

Were they right about ending the animosity with Brody? Every nerve in her body was telling her she'd made a big mistake. She should have stood her ground.

Easier said than done.

Chapter Ten

"Mr. Hawkins has been waiting over fifteen minutes," Mrs. Kingston chided. She walked over and fluffed out the yards of hand-embroidered lavender silk of Sara's skirt. "He's going to wear out the carpet with his pacing. Are you planning to stay in your room for the rest of the evening?"

Sara wanted to scream. She hadn't liked the new housekeeper from the day she first arrived, and at this moment she liked her even less because she was right. She couldn't stay in her bedroom forever.

Sara accepted the gloves Mrs. Kingston handed her and immediately dropped them. Embarrassed, she reached down and picked them up before Mrs. Kingston could.

Ever since agreeing to accompany Brody Hawkins to the ball, she had become all thumbs. She dropped everything she touched and constantly bumped into things, like the corner of her desk at work. If only he hadn't made the comment about their coupling being inevitable and that it was simply a matter of time. Would it be tonight? Would she be able to withstand him?

Now the dreaded evening had arrived and she did not want to go downstairs. Plus Mrs. Kingston had the audacity to be mouthy! Why couldn't the woman understand that Sara was harboring very serious doubts about the evening?

Sara took a stabilizing breath. She'd done quite well in the past at acting as if his nearness had no effect on her. But she knew she'd never be able to pull it off tonight. Did she even want to? How long could she resist a man like Brody?

All she had to do was think about what she'd gone through with Malcolm Speck. The man who'd tried to sell her father's company out from under her.

Hadn't he taught her a very valuable lesson about men? Just the thought of him helped fortify her decision to act the perfect, aloof lady. She would certainly not lower herself to become one of the women who fawned all over Mr. Hawkins.

Sara raised her chin. She might as well get this over with. Teeth clenched, she headed for the door. Tomorrow everything would look much brighter.

As Sara descended the flight of stairs, her gaze fastened on the man waiting below. He looked devastatingly handsome in his tailored evening clothes, and all the more devilish.

"You are truly a beautiful woman," Brody complimented, as he held out his hand to her.

"How gracious of you." Inwardly Sara congratulated herself on her apparent composure while her insides were turning to mush. Thank heavens for long skirts, that prevented him from seeing her knees knocking.

"I'm sorry I kept you waiting."

"Good things come to those who wait."

Sara took a deep breath, as Brody placed her cloak over her shoulders, then opened the door and led her out into the cool evening.

The stars danced in Sara's eyes upon seeing the burgundy carriage he'd brought. It glistened in the moonlight. He seemed to have plucked it from a fairy tale. There were even a coachman and footman dressed in matching coats of burgundy and gold.

As they approached, the footman lowered the step for her use. Sara felt every inch a queen. Especially when she sank into the soft leather seat.

"I've never traveled in such luxury," Sara admitted.

"I use the carriage for long trips, like when I travel to Washington. I thought you'd find it warmer and more comfortable. There are blankets in the boot should you get too cold."

"Have you ever met the president?" she asked.

The carriage pulled away from the house.

"On many occasions."

Sara was impressed. She'd known he was a man of substance, but not so important that he mingled with presidents.

"Mr. Hawkins—"

"Brody."

"Brody. Since you have gone to the trouble of arranging tonight's outing, perhaps you would like to inform me as to what you expect of me."

"Nothing."

"Nothing?"

"That's right, nothing."

Sara fell silent and listened to the beat of the horses' hooves striking the bricked street. The carriage seats were wide, and though she was close enough to smell Brody's spicy shaving lotion, there was enough room for another person to sit between them. This helped to soothe her nerves. Brody's attitude also helped. Other than the compliment he'd given her in the house, he'd remained the perfect gentleman.

"Are you still angry at being forced to accompany me tonight?"

Sara tensed. She wished she could see his face, but it was dark inside the carriage. "I'll tell you when the night is over." She heard his soft chuckle.

"Then I must dedicate myself to making it especially enjoyable for you. Tonight we'll just be two people out for a pleasant evening. And who knows? We may even get to know each other better." Brody smiled, knowing she couldn't see him.

"In turn, I'll do what I can to squelch any rumors of misconduct on your part."

"Thank you," Brody replied.

The rest of the distance was traveled in silence.

Sara still hadn't recovered from learning that Brody knew the President of the United States. He'd said that if he'd wanted to close her down, the situation would have already been taken care of. She hadn't believed him then, but she believed him now.

Nallie Wooten stood with her son, Otis, and daughter-in-law, Rose, welcoming her guests. When Sara and Brody approached her, Sara was certain the older woman's smile broadened to the size of a sitting room.

"I'm so happy you came," Nallie said, a bit too loud. "And Sara, your gown is going to make every woman jealous." She winked at Brody. "That and being escorted by Mr. Hawkins."

Otis and Brody shook hands. "You're just the man I need to see. I fear the freighting business is fixing to come to a halt. There are all sorts of rumors flying around about the railroad moving west."

"Otis!" Nallie spat out. "There will be no talk about business tonight!"

"Mother Wooten is right, dear." Rose patted her husband's arm.

"I'll talk to you later, Brody."

The worried look on Otis's face left Sara wondering if there was reason for concern.

After passing the receiving line, Brody turned to Sara. "I do believe the orchestra is playing a waltz." His eyes glistened with humor as he held out his arm. "Shall we try?"

"I'd be delighted." Sara stepped into his embrace, eager to show how her dancing had improved.

As they glided around the dance floor, Brody turned her in various moves that she had never experienced before. But not once did she stumble or step on his foot. His smile of approval was her compliment.

Sara quickly learned why, besides his good looks, women clung to Brody's every word. Like most men, he was attentive and didn't wander off. But Brody carried it a step further.

As he had undoubtedly done with many others, he made her feel as if she were the only woman in the room he cared to be with. Not with words or lavish gestures. His eyes never roamed, and when they visited with mutual friends, he made a point of including her in the conversation. While engaged in a conversation about horses, about which she knew little, he'd suddenly look at her and smiled, as if to say he hadn't forgotten she was there.

The gentleman did indeed know how to treat a lady.

"You look as if you're having a wonderful time," Clara said excitedly.

Sara had joined the Baronesses while waiting for

Brody to fetch her drink. They were seated on their usual chairs which Sara had learned were transported from place to place as needed.

"And she is," Nallie assured Clara. "Sara, you should have known we would never have you do anything with Brody that would bring on more conflict."

"We knew you were upset with us for making you promise to come with him tonight." Harriet giggled. "But we also knew that you don't know him as well as we do. He's such a gentleman."

Clara nodded. "And a rogue."

"Absolutely," Bertha chimed in. "That's the part that makes him so interesting."

Sara broke out laughing. How could anyone stay angry with these women? "Have you noticed that not a single man has asked me to dance?" she asked. "Don't you find that strange?"

"No man with an ounce of brain would dare." Clara brushed a wayward strand of gray hair from her face.

"Why? Because he's rich? The truth be known, I have the suspicion he's a bit of a coward." She looked around the room. When she caught a man's eye, he quickly looked away. She was about to break protocol and ask Curtis Farmington to dance when she felt a hand on her arm. It was Clara's.

"You wouldn't want to spoil Nallie's grand ball, would you? I understand your feelings. I used to be every bit as high-spirited as you are. But I learned the hard way to control my urges."

Of the four women, Clara had always been the one Sara felt closest to. Seeing the other three were in deep conversation, Sara leaned over so Clara could hear her lowered voice. "Do you really believe Brody would do something if I were to dance with another man?"

"Probably not. Gentlemen do not make scenes. But I can't say he wouldn't have a talk with the man at a later time."

"Animals are supposed to be territorial," Sara whispered out the corner of her mouth, "not humans."

"Oh, my dear, you have so much to learn. Humans are animals."

Brody brought Sara her drink, and they stood talking with the elderly women until she'd finished it. As they moved onto the dance floor, Clara caught sight of her daughter-in-law headed in her direction. She signed discontentedly.

"Mother Riggs," Patricia called, even before reaching Clara's side. "Can you tell me why on earth Brody chose to accompany Sara here?"

"Brody doesn't confide such things to me. However, she's a very beautiful woman. Just look at the two of them dancing. Don't they epitomize the future of Kansas."

"Oh!"

Patricia stormed off and Clara laughed.

* * *

It was nearing three in the morning when the carriage arrived at Sara's home. She'd had the most wonderful night of her life, and she didn't want it to end.

"I doubt that there will be any more rumors about you mistreating me."

Brody shifted so he could look toward her. "Thanks to you."

"Does that mean we now have a truce?"

"Absolutely. If you're willing, we could even be friends."

"Then friends it shall be. Besides, I don't like having to shoot at people."

Brody's rich laughter filled the carriage. "I wouldn't advise it."

The carriage stopped. The footman opened the door and helped Sara down. Brody escorted her to her front door.

"Thank you for a most enjoyable evening." Brody raised her hand and kissed her knuckles.

Sara had been ready for a kiss, but not on her hand. "I enjoyed it also." At a loss as to what to say, she opened the door slightly. She hesitated, hoping he'd changed his mind about kissing her on the lips.

To Sara's disappointment, Brody tipped his top hat and returned to the coach.

Sara entered the silent house, closed the door and leaned against it. All evening she had thought about Brody kissing her good-night and how she would make it into the house before surrendering to him. But nothing had happened.

"Do you want to soil your reputation?" Mrs. Kingston snapped as she turned up the lantern. "Proper women do not linger and allow men to kiss them good-night. Now, come upstairs. I'll help you slip off your gown and put your nightdress on."

"He didn't kiss me good-night!" Sara replied curtly.

"Good. Perhaps the man has some redeeming qualities after all."

The housekeeper headed for the stairs, but Sara didn't follow. "Mrs. Kingston," she called as she slid the cape from her shoulders.

Mrs. Kingston stopped on the third step and turned.

"You haven't any right to tell me what to do or how I should act."

Mrs. Kingston's cheeks puffed out in indignation. "Women like you need proper guidance. You'd be wise to heed what I say."

The woman's brash tongue infuriated Sara. After all the trouble Patricia had gone to find the solemn-faced woman, Sara had hesitated to fire her. But enough was enough. "I no longer have any need for your services. I will expect you to be moved from these premises by noon tomorrow."

The older woman's face turned crimson. "You can't fire me! I was hired by Mrs. Riggs."

"And who pays your wages?"

"I have the very best of references."

"You have until noon tomorrow." Sara started up the stairs, brushing past the housekeeper.

"I'll report this to Mrs. Riggs," Mrs. Kingston threatened as Sara continued on her way. "She'll set you straight."

Sara entered her room, slamming the door behind her. The nerve of the woman, she thought, as she flung her cape over the back of a chair. With no one to help her undress, the task took longer than usual, but she would have eaten worms rather than call Mrs. Kingston.

By the time Sara had her nightdress on, her temper had cooled. She would not let Mrs. Kingston ruin her evening.

She waltzed around the room, pretending she was with Brody. Finally she jumped onto the bed, sank in the feather mattress and looked up at the ceiling. She touched the back of her hand where Brody had kissed it, trying to recapture the sensation of his lips on her skin.

A soft groan worked its way past her throat. What was Brody doing to her? If only she had someone to advise her. But her dearest friends were also smitten with him and could see no wrong. She didn't dare talk to Patricia. From the moment she and Brody had arrived at the ball, Patricia's eyes had flashed daggers.

Sara had no need to ask why. Patricia had been jealous. Realizing that, Sara remembered all the bad things Patricia had said about Brody and how she'd gone out of her way to keep them apart.

Sara had been proud of the way she'd kept her reserve and maintained a degree of aloofness tonight. Not once had she reacted to Brody as she'd seen other women do. She wasn't overly attentive, and though she'd felt his smiles all the way to her toes, he wasn't aware of it.

However, her inward battle was taking its toll. Even at this moment, she ached for him; longed to know what it was like to have him kiss her, make love to her. She had wanted him to lead her down the path to passion.

Sara sighed. Though she did a lot of fantasizing, she would have definitely resisted any advances Brody might have made. Why did she continue to fight her desire? Because she knew that if she allowed him to make love to her, he'd settle for nothing less than her very soul. She was already falling in love with him. When he decided to leave her for another woman, her heart would surely break.

And he *would* leave her. Brody Hawkins had never loved a woman. Perhaps he wasn't even capable of loving.

The cold room raised gooseflesh. Sara quickly climbed beneath the covers. "You spend too much time contemplating," she chided herself.

Keeping her relationship with Brody strictly a friendship was the wisest solution. For now.

Chapter Eleven

Sara shoved the shipping papers across the desk and waited for Lucas to look at them.

"Four outfits going out again," Lucas hollered jubilantly. "You've done it, Sara! Just like you said you would."

Sara laughed. "And next year we're going to do even better. But I couldn't have accomplished it without you, Lucas."

"Nonsense."

"Therefore, I have decided to give you one percent of the company profits.'

"No."

"Like it or not, I'm going to make you a wealthy man. Before long you'll find yourself a woman, get married and be raising children."

Lucas lowered his eyes and grinned, his white teeth gleaming against his sun-darkened skin. It was the first time Sara had seen him blush.

"And how about you, missy? When you aimin' to get married and have babies?"

"I'm thinking about going into a convent."

Lucas shook his head. "It'll never happen."

Several weeks later, Sara left the bank building feeling quite euphoric. Mr. Dibble, the bank president, had just spent a good thirty minutes praising her for all she had accomplished and assuring her the bank doors would always be open.

It was a splendid summer's day, and as Sara strolled along the walk looking in store windows, her pace slowed. Strange that this was the first time she'd walked downtown since moving to Leavenworth. It used to be her favorite pastime when living in Atchison.

She paused a moment to look at some dishes on display. Life is such a contradiction, she thought. Now that she had money, she couldn't spend it. Most of it had to be put back into the company. Not having several solid years behind her forced her to wait until she could estimate what her average yearly cost would be.

"Greetings."

To Sara's surprise, Brody Hawkins stood only a few feet ahead. Instead of a suit, he wore a white full-sleeved shirt and tight black trousers that stretched across a set of muscular thighs. He looked very powerful, his chest broad and muscular.

"Are you waiting for someone?" she asked, stopping in front of him.

"I'm waiting for you. I decided this was a perfect day for us to have a picnic."

A mischievous look had entered his eyes. "I don't believe that for a minute." With his back to the sun, she had to squint to see his face.

"You should, it's true. I was on my way to your office when I caught sight of you walking this way."

Sara grinned. His clothes were more suited for a devilish pirate. Surely he had just stepped out of a storybook. "And pray tell, how many will be attending this picnic?"

"Just the two of us. Are you interested?

Sara looked up at the sky. "It is a beautiful day."

"Then let's be off."

"I really should take you up on the offer just to see how you manage to squirm out of it."

He took her by the elbow and led her to the buggy parked a few feet away. With a grin stretching from ear to ear, he leaned over and raised a wide napkin covering the top of a deep wicker basket. Though she didn't get a good look at the contents, there really was food inside.

"You're actually serious!"

"Absolutely."

"But why?" was all she could think to say.

"One good turn deserves another. You did me a favor by attending the summer ball and I'm reciprocating. After all, what are friends for? We are still friends, aren't we?''

"Of course, but..."

He replaced the napkin. "Just the other day, Nallie Wooten made a comment about you spending far too much time working.''

"That's not so. Besides, I'm running a business,'' she stated defensively. He'd moved again and she had to shadow her eyes with her hand against the sun.

"So do I, but I also find time for other pleasures.''

Sara wasn't about to pursue that particular conversation.

"Come on, Sara, let's have a picnic.''

"I don't know,'' she hesitated.

"You're obviously not a woman who does things on the spur of the moment. We'll have to change that. Believe me, it's a lot more enjoyable.''

His lightheartedness was contagious. Still, Sara hesitated. The thought of going with him was pleasing, but she had to guard her heart and keep her feet firmly on the ground. "No, there are things I need to take care of.''

"I thought we agreed to be friends?'' He shook his head. "I can't believe that you're so fickle you've already changed your mind? I promise to behave myself.''

Brody's charm was outweighed Sara's caution. "I've heard you can be a dangerous man.''

"I'll try to be on my best behavior." He took her arm again. "I'll help you into the buggy."

"We won't be gone long, will we?"

"We'll head back the minute you say so."

"I'll have to stop by the office to let them know I won't be in," Sara said as she settled onto the buggy seat, "and I'll need to go home and change clothes."

Brody untied the short rope from the tethering post and climbed onto the other side of Sara. Instead of heading on down the street, he turned the horse in the opposite direction.

"What are you doing?" Sara demanded.

"If you're going to learn to do things on the spur of the moment, you need to know that preparations are definitely not part of it."

"But I have to—"

"Didn't you just comment on what a beautiful day it is? We need to take advantage of such weather."

By not stopping at the office, Sara felt like a child doing something naughty, and thoroughly enjoyed it. And this would be a perfect time to get to know more about her friend. "Do you come from a wealthy family?" she asked Brody.

"Why would you ask that?"

"You're used to getting what you want. That takes money." Receiving nothing but a grunt, she continued on. "Why did you choose freighting as an occupation?"

"As you once so eloquently pointed out, there is

lots of money to be made in freighting. Now it's my turn to ask a question.''

Sara's eyes mirrored her curiosity. ''But you haven't answered mine. You're deliberately being evasive. I haven't learned a thing about you.'' She caught sight of a paddle wheeler coming up river. There were so many people and goods aboard that it was a wonder it didn't sink. ''It seems everyone is headed west,'' she commented thoughtfully. ''I heard tell that covered wagons are being ordered faster than they can be built.''

''I have a feeling that we're only seeing the start of it.''

''You sound excited.''

Brody nodded. ''Times are changing, Sara. Part of me wants to pack up and go with them.''

Sara knew she had just seen a side of Brody she'd likely never see again. She'd been right. He did have an adventuresome spirit.

Sara suddenly realized they were headed toward the ferry. Where did he plan on taking her? He may have acted the gentleman at the ball, but she still didn't trust being alone with him, especially in the wilderness. She had made a mistake by accepting his invitation.

Another thought came to mind. He'd made sure no one knew that she'd left with him. ''I do not care to go on the other side of the river,'' she said, her concern mounting.

Brody already had the nervous horse moving onto

the ferry. Once they were on board, he climbed down to hold the horse steady.

"I'm not going," Sara stated firmly as she started to climb from the rig. But the ferry lurched, and she had to grab the side of the seat to keep from falling.

"Be careful," Brody warned.

She settled back into the seat, her eyes glued to the other side of the river.

"If you want to get down, I'll help you."

His straight, white teeth were a contrast to a face darkened by wind and sun. "No, I'm just a bit nervous."

"Surely you're not skittish about crossing the river?" Brody teased.

"No, it's not that…I mean—" The thick ropes were already being pulled, and the ferry had left shore.

Brody stood waiting for her to finish her sentence. "If you don't want to see where I'd planned on taking you," he finally said, "just say so and we'll take the ferry back."

He paid the ferryman.

Sara felt guilty. She acted the snit while he chose to be nice. He probably wasn't even guilty of the sordid thoughts that came to mind. "No," she said hesitantly, "that won't be necessary. Clara Riggs and the others have always said you—" she couldn't point out her suspicions to him "—are the best friend a person could want. I just thought we'd have our picnic in some park."

His smile widened in approval. "I've picked a far more secluded spot. Parks seem to always be a bit crowded. Don't you think?"

"I haven't been to one lately." Sara looked at the approaching shore. It wasn't too late to tell him she'd changed her mind...again.

"I'm glad you don't want to go back." Brody caressed the horse's muzzle. "Where we're going is only a short distance from the landing."

In a near state of panic, Sara retrieved a handkerchief from beneath her sleeve and dabbed her damp forehead. Malcolm had made her distrustful of men, but Brody seemed to be the only one she worried about.

"You'd be a lot cooler if you removed your jacket," Brody commented.

The ferry landed and Brody climbed back onto the buggy. A slight flick of the reins started the horse forward.

Once on land, Brody insisted on helping Sara slip out of her short jacket. Sara placed it between them, wondering why she had allowed Brody to continue on. If anything happened, it would be her own fault.

"How much farther are we going?" Realizing she was fidgeting with a tuck in her skirt, she stopped.

"We're just about there."

Brody turned onto what looked like an old trail

lined with trees and thick bushes. Sara's nervousness increased.

"Did your father or brother ever take you on the trail?" Brody asked.

Sara hardly heard the question. "No. As much as I pleaded, they would never allow it." She wrung her hands. "Do you plan on stopping anytime soon?"

"Around the next bend. Why, Sara, you're shaking. You needn't worry about anything. You're with me."

Sara wanted to laugh. *He* was her concern. "Why would you say something like that? I'm not at all frightened."

Sara's misgivings suited Brody. He wanted her to feel a sense of nervousness. That way he'd remain in her thoughts.

Sara felt considerably better when, true to his word, Brody brought the horse to a halt in a small glade with an old widespread tree in the middle and splotches of thick green grass covering the ground. About twenty feet away, the river lapped gently onto a tiny beach. It was peaceful...and very romantic.

"How did you ever find this place?" Sara asked as he helped her from the buggy. The touch of his hand made her want to pick her feet up and run.

"It's my secret fishing hole."

"Your what?" Had she heard him correctly?

"Have you ever been fishing?" He took the basket and a quilt from the boot of the buggy and headed for the tree.

"No." While she'd been concerned about his un-wanted attentions, he had been thinking about fishing?

"What a shame. I guess I'm just going to have to teach you."

Instead of stopping under the tree, Brody continued on to the bank.

"Hold this." He handed her the basket. After spreading out the quilt, he walked back to the buggy.

Sara sat on a corner of the quilt, making sure not to get any grass stains on her skirt.

A moment later, Brody returned with two long poles, cord and an old can. Curious, Sara watched as he tied the twine to the poles. That was followed with hooks, which were secured onto the other end of the line. Sara had never been fishing, but during her younger days, her playmate, Tommy, used to go all the time. He'd return home and tell her all about it and show off his catch.

Sara scrunched her face as Brody pulled out a fat worm from the can and skewered it with a hook. A piece of metal was used for a weight. He did the same on the other hook.

"Are you ready?"

Sara narrowed her eyes. "What do you mean, am I ready?"

"To throw your line into the water. How else are we going to catch fish? As long as we're going to be friends, we might as well learn to do what the other likes."

"I don't like to fish," Sara stated firmly.

"You can't say that. You've never tried it." He walked to the edge of the water. "I guess I've been all wrong about you."

"What do you mean?"

"I didn't think you'd be the type to worry about getting her hands dirty, or that you'd be so judgmental about something you've never tried."

Even though Sara knew he'd been goading her, like a fool she chose to take the bait. She would not give him more ammunition to pick at her.

She walked to where he stood and grimaced at the feel of her shoes sinking into the soft mud. "What am I supposed to do?"

"You're going to take hold of the end of the pole with both hands and you're going to cast the line out into the water as far as you can." He demonstrated, with the end of the line dropping into the water a good distance away.

"Now, it's your turn."

Sara cast it out as far as Brody had.

"Are you sure you've never done this before?" Brody asked, still puzzled at the distance she had managed. She was so small that the feat seemed impossible. Then he remembered being told she knew how to use a whip.

"Quite sure." Sara's stomach rumbled. It had to be after one o'clock, and she hadn't eaten all day. She was about to suggest food when her pole was almost yanked from her hands.

Sara turned to Brody, her brown eyes as big as moons. "I think I've caught something!"

"No. It's probably just—" He watched the end of the pole bend downward.

"What am I supposed to do?" Sara asked. "Here, you take it!"

"No, no. It's your catch. Start pulling in the line." How could she have caught a fish that quickly? Brody wondered.

Brody paused a moment before yanking off his boots and wading into water to help her pull the line in...something he would definitely have preferred not doing. He hadn't gone far when Sara appeared alongside him. He stopped upon seeing her excitement and wide grin. The lady had every intention of landing the fish by herself.

Brody gladly retreated and took a seat on the dry part of the bank, amazed at what he was seeing. Sara, shoes and all, stood nearly knee deep in water, her skirt soaked up to her tiny waist. The lady might look small and fragile, but she was a tiger.

"I've still got it!" Sara said excitedly. "What do I do now?"

"Bring it onto the shore."

Brody chuckled when Sara suddenly realized how far she'd waded out. Still, undaunted, she moved forward, dragging her line and skirt, which had now stretched into a train.

As the water became shallower, the effort to tow the heavy material onto dry land increased. On land, the drenched hem being dragged across the dirt, turned the ground quickly into mud, and the mud attached itself to the material making the skirt twice as heavy. When she came to a halt beside him, she had left behind a perfectly swept path and a fish flopping about.

"Where is *your* fish?" Sara challenged.

Brody shooed a fly away. Not only had Sara caught a fish right away, it came close to being the biggest he had ever seen. "My line is still in the river," he replied dryly. "Usually it takes some time before a fish takes the bait."

Sara knew by his tone of voice that he wasn't particularly pleased at being bested. "I didn't have any trouble," she bragged. "Are we going to cook it?"

"I have nothing to cook it in. You'll have to put it back into the water."

Sara gasped. "After all I just went through?" She glanced around the area. "You don't plan things very well, do you? Since you wanted to fish, how did you intend to cook our catch? You've obviously done little camping. Well, don't worry, I know exactly what to do."

Brody drew his knees up and, wrapping his arms around them watched in awe. Sara had actually started to gather dead wood. "That won't be necessary," he informed her.

Intent on what she was doing, Sara didn't hear him. "When I was young, Papa had a scout we called Indian Bob. When Papa wasn't around, I'd get Bob to teach me all sorts of things. He taught me how to build a fire and how to cook on it. You wouldn't believe how many fires I started."

"Sara, a catfish can't be cooked until it's skinned. If you don't want to throw it back, I'll tie it on a string and place it back in the water so it'll stay fresh. You can take it home to your cook." He raised his brows. "Unless you also know how to make a knife."

"No," Sara replied seriously. "I had thought to spear it through the middle with a green branch. But if it has to be skinned..." She dropped the sticks.

Brody saw no reason to tell her about the knife he always kept strapped to his leg. He leaned over and removed the hook from the fish's mouth. After stringing a sturdy cord through the fish's gills and securing one end around a fairly good-size rock, he tossed the fish back into the water.

So much for a leisurely afternoon of fishing.

"Are we through?" Sara asked when he started pulling in his line.

"Yep."

"Why? We might catch more."

"What would we do with them? You have a big one to take home and I don't want to take any back.

And, at the rate you're going, we'd probably end up with a whole bucket full of them.''

"I suppose you're right."

Brody grinned at Sara's obvious disappointment. The woman would never make a good gambler. Her large brown eyes were too expressive.

"Besides, we haven't had our picnic and you need to get dried off." He took the fishing pole from her hands and put it with his on the ground.

Sara looked down at her skirt. It was totally ruined, but catching her first fish had made it worth it. She hadn't had so much fun in years.

"You should take your skirt and petticoats off and drape them over the bush behind you. The sun will help dry them."

"I will not. I can manage fine without going to such extremes."

"Suit yourself."

That wasn't what Sara had expected to hear. She watched him go over and make himself comfortable on the quilt. Where was she going to sit? She'd make a holy mess if she were to join him. Her stomach growled. The thick slice of ham he'd pulled from the basket was too tempting. Saliva filled her mouth as she watched him take a big, juicy bite.

"Are you just going to stand there and watch me?" Brody asked.

"No...no, I was just trying to decide where I should sit." She lifted her skirt, only to have her arms coated with the thick mud the material had collected. Frustrated, she tried wiping them off on a clean spot in front of her skirt, but ended up getting that area muddy, also.

Brody could no longer contain his laughter as he watched Sara's situation go from bad to worse. Aggravated, she unthinkingly wiped a hand across her cheek, leaving half her face smeared. Thoroughly enjoying himself, he took another bite of the honey-baked ham then tore a piece off the fresh loaf of bread.

When Brody looked up, Sara was staring at the bread in his hand. She licked her lip, as if tasting the food. Again he reached inside the basket, broke off a piece of cheese, then popped it into his mouth. "There's even pie in the basket," he commented.

"How can you sit there and eat?" Sara demanded. Though she'd moved to a patch of grass, the stomp of her foot sent mud flying.

"What else would you have me do? In case you forgot, permit me to remind you that this was supposed to be a picnic." He opened a bottle of red wine.

"Do you actually think I would undress in front of you? I think not!" She plopped down on the grass. "Besides, I had a big breakfast and I'm not hungry. I'll just sit here until you're ready to go."

"I have another quilt in the boot that you could put around you while your dress and underskirts dry."

"No. And it's extremely ungentlemanly to be discussing my underclothing."

His deep laughter filled the air and Sara's temper flared.

"You needn't worry about me attacking you," he managed to say between peal of laughter. "I'm not particularly fond of muddy affairs."

Sara looked down at her dress, suddenly realizing what she must look like. One big blob of mud. It was probably even in her hair. Still, he had no right to laugh at her!

Sara gave him a cynical smile before standing. She then moved to the quilt and plopped down. In a most ladylike fashion, she picked up a delicate white linen napkin and proceeded to wipe her hands. Another napkin was used on her face. "I solved my own problem."

Her hands still stained with dry mud, Sara grabbed the piece of ham from his hand, her eyes defying him to say something. The smile that remained on his face and that confounded all-knowing look in his eyes was the straw that broke the camel's back.

As she took another bite, she sneaked her other hand behind her and collected a handful of mud from her skirt. Before he could guess what she was up to, Sara flung it at him. It hit Brody on the side of his face, right where she'd aimed it. Another handful quickly followed, hitting his chest and splattering his once-white shirt.

Sara would never have thought so big a man could move so fast. She had no sooner released the glob of mud than a retaliating handful of mud landed on her face. ''Not fair,'' she stated.

''Not fair that I should return what I so graciously received?'' His hand was poised, just waiting for her to deliver another blow.

''Not fair that you have bigger hands than I do.''

''I'm being every bit the gentleman. I allowed you two to my one.''

Sara giggled. As he spoke, mud slid down his cheek and onto his clothes. They both broke out laughing.

''I quit,'' she finally gasped, then fell backward onto the grass, holding her sore ribs from laughing so hard.

Brody couldn't remember ever having had a more unconventional outing, and certainly not with a totally feminine tomboy. In fact, he'd never met a totally feminine tomboy before. He had to admire Sara's ability to laugh at herself, and her lack of need to put on airs. Most women would be screaming their heads off if just one tiny drop of water had touched them.

''I don't know about you,'' Brody said when their laughter had subsided, ''but I'm hungry.''

''That makes two of us. Mmm. I smell chicken,'' she commented as she gazed expectantly at what Brody was unveiling in the large basket. ''I hope you're not one of those men who believe the man should eat first,'' she chided.

''And if I am?''

''You shall have a fight on your hands.'' Sara licked

her lips upon seeing a whole baked chicken revealed.
She was so hungry she could probably eat the entire
bird by herself.

"No need. To show you what a gentleman I am,
I'll let you have the first choice. Light meat or dark?"
Brody was quite pleased with the day's outing. Sara
had finally relaxed in his company. Exactly the way
he'd planned it. That wasn't quite true. A mud fight
had accomplished it.

Sara looked up from her work, surprised to see
Brody standing before her desk. For the past week
she'd spent hours each morning deliberating on just
the right town suit to wear, how to arrange her hair,
just in hopes of seeing him.

"Good morning."

Now that the handsome gentleman had arrived, Sara
became tongue-tied. She nodded. Her smile seemed
glued to her face. She had never known a man who
could mesmerize her with just one look.

Brody's mouth twitched with humor. "Are we talking today or have you developed laryngitis from over-
exposure to mud?"

Sara's smile widened. "No," she finally managed
to say, "I'm not suffering from laryngitis. It's just nice
to see…a friend in the middle of the morning. And
there is no mud." She stood, stepped away from the
desk and turned so he could see for himself.

"Ah, yes. I must say there is a bit of an improvement. Your green-and-white suit is far more becoming.''

Though embarrassed by his leisurely perusal, the compliment pleased Sara all the way to her toes. "And you, sir, have a very fine tailor."

Brody bowed his head. "I'll tell him."

"Won't you sit down? To what do I owe the pleasure of your visit? Obviously you're not planning on going fishing today." This was the first friendly visit they'd had in her office, and she was enjoying every minute.

"Unfortunately I can't stay long. Like you, I have meetings and other necessary projects to attend to. However, I'm going to be at my ranch over the weekend, and I thought you might accompany me for a visit."

"Your ranch?" Sara would never have suspected him of being a rancher. He didn't even know the fundamentals of making a fire and his dress, home and manners had led her to believe he preferred spending his time in town. But he did like to fish.

"I have a spread in Missouri, some twenty miles from here. I thought you'd enjoy spending the weekend there."

"With you?"

"Of course with me."

"This weekend?"

"Yes."

"Alone?"

Brody rubbed his chin. Her eyes seemed to enlarge with each sentence she spoke. "I thought it would be a bit far for you to go back and forth in one day. We won't be entirely alone. I do have servants."

Sara gulped. Warning signs were going up again. Unthinkingly, she moved behind her desk. "I don't—"

"Are we going to go through this again?" Brody placed his hand on the back of the chair in front of him. "Sara, when are you going to learn to trust me? If I intended to ravish you I could have done so when I took you to the ball or when we went fishing. Perhaps I should say when *you* went fishing."

His tease returned Sara's good mood. But once again he had managed to put her in a difficult position. She couldn't truly distrust him. Other than one kiss, he had never touched her.

"I couldn't possibly go. People would talk and I certainly don't want a bad reputation. I've worked hard to be respected by the community."

"No one need know," he said softly. "I seldom take anyone there."

Sara didn't believe that other women hadn't received the same invitation. Even so, just being asked thrilled her. The romantic pictures that leaped into her head were enough to make her swoon. Which was exactly why she had to refuse...until a thought came to mind.

"You're right about my suspicious nature. I have

nothing to base it on. Therefore I accept your invitation."

"Good. I'll be in front of your house early Saturday morning." He started toward the door, then stopped. "Do you ever go horseback riding?"

"Yes, but it's been years, and I have no horse to ride." Feeling much safer, Sara came from behind her desk again. "Don't bother coming for me. I'm not sure when I'll be ready and I'd much rather drive my own buggy. If you'll just have your clerk bring me the directions, I'll do just fine."

"It's a long way," he replied smoothly, though she was obviously still wary about being alone with him.

"I've traveled farther."

"Very well. Until Saturday."

As Brody walked out onto the sidewalk, he wondered how long it would take for Sara to stop shying away from him. But all along, getting her to come to him willingly had been part of the challenge.

Of course, if he were any kind of a gentleman, he'd back off. But once he'd stepped into the water he'd had every intention of taking a swim. Each time he saw Sara Miles, his determination grew. Come what may, he would possess her.

Sara plopped down in her chair, her breathing slowly returning to normal. Every part of her throbbed. She had become as susceptible to Brody's looks and charm as the other women who clung to him. There was, however, one big glaring difference. He'd seemed only interested in being her friend.

Sara rubbed the back of her neck. He was a handsome, virile man, so why would he not be interested in her as a woman? She shook her head. Since their truce, Brody hadn't said or done a thing that would indicate he wanted her in his bed. Yet she continued to run scared. That little thread of suspicion kept nagging at her.

She felt perfectly in control with other men, but not Brody. She had no idea what went on in his mind but behind those green eyes there was a promise of fulfilled dreams. That's what had her worried. The way he walked, talked and even moved showed he had no doubts about his prowess in bed. And what if she succumbed like the others before her? It chilled her to think of how it would eventually end.

Sara placed her elbows on the desk and rested her head in her hands. She had to be a crazy. Why else would she continue to torture herself by being around Brody?

After her stay at the ranch, she would tell Brody she never wanted to see him again. She suddenly snatched up her reticule and left the office. She had a visit to make.

Chapter Twelve

Brody stood on the porch of his house talking to his foreman when he spied dust rising in the distance. It had to be Sara. A single rider's horse didn't leave that wide a trail. Besides, he wasn't expecting any other guests.

"Is there anything else we need to discuss, Red?"

"Nope, reckon not." The foreman slapped his hat across his leg to knock out the dust. A band of sweat circled the crown from years of wear. "I'm curious about one thing."

"What's that?" Brody stepped down from the porch, Red following. He hadn't expected Sara to arrive so early. Dare he hope she was anxious to see him? Anticipation wasn't wise. With Sara nothing seemed to go the way it should.

"What you aimin' to do with that mare that was delivered yesterday? She's as fine an animal as they come. I'd be willing to buy her from you."

"Too late. She already belongs to the lady coming down the road, though she doesn't know it yet."

Like Brody, Red stood watching the dust kicking into the slight wind. "I should of known."

"Besides, what do you need with another horse?"

"I ain't got one like that."

The two men grinned and Red took off toward the bunkhouse.

Though Brody knew it would be another fifteen minutes before Sara arrived at the ranch house, he tipped his hat back and waited.

For a brief moment, the buggy came into view then disappeared behind a tree. Brody thought he'd seen two people on the seat. It had to be the sun playing tricks on him. He cupped his hand over his brow as the conveyance came around the bend. It was definitely Sara. He'd recognize that broom-tail horse anywhere. And he'd been right. There were two people. Sara and Clara Riggs.

The little vixen had brought along a chaperon. Why wasn't he surprised?

Brody gave the two women a welcoming smile as Sara brought the horse to a halt. Her bright eyes darted from one place to another as if trying to take everything in at once. Brody looped the reins around the hitching post then went around to help Clara down.

"How nice of you to accompany Sara," he said as he took her hand. "I worried about her driving all this distance without a chaperon."

"It was thoughtful of you to suggest it."

Brody glanced at Sara who had already stepped down. She shrugged her shoulders, her smile growing wider by the minute.

"I've heard about this place for years and have been dying to come out," Clara continued.

"You should have said something," Brody patronized. "Henceforth you have an open invitation."

"You're such a dear boy." Clara turned and looked at the house. "Oh, this brings back such memories, but your log home is much bigger than the one my dear Homer built when we first came out here. And I always wanted a wraparound porch like yours, where I could sit in my rocker and watch the sun set!"

"You must be exhausted after traveling so far. Let's go inside so you can freshen up.

As Sara followed along, she also admired the large one-story structure. She hadn't expected something so big.

Her admiration quickly shifted to its owner. He looked so different with his wide-brimmed hat, his shirt open at the neck and his sleeves rolled up his strong forearms. The tight-fitting jeans molded over a small behind and made her feel like some twittering female. It was enough to send any warm-blooded woman's head reeling.

Be careful, Sara warned herself. You're treading a very dangerous ground. She had been right to bring Clara along.

Sara walked up the three steps and crossed the wide porch. Again she vowed that after tomorrow, she would never see Brody again. She was tired of fighting temptation, and Brody was indeed tempting. There was no question that if she wanted to play with fire, she'd eventually get burned.

Sara found the inside of the house refreshingly cool. She removed her straw hat and glanced around the large room. The comfortable leather sofas, large chairs and Indian rugs adorning the polished wooden floors seemed to welcome her. Even the Indian artifacts on one wall and heavy oak end tables added to the overall ambience. The room was completely opposite from the decor of his home in town. Brody Hawkins was a man of contradictions.

A slender, very attractive woman entered the room and stood waiting. Though she wore a clean calico dress, her long black braids and darker skin made her Indian heritage apparent. Sara's twinge of jealousy came unexpectedly.

"Ladies, this is Kapata, my housekeeper. She'll show you to your rooms. Unfortunately she speaks very little English. When you feel rested, we'll have lunch and then, if you feel up to it, I'll give you a quick tour of my ranch."

Sara didn't want to rest, but they had left early that morning and after their long journey, Clara probably needed to lie down for a bit. Sara followed the two women, hoping Clara's nap wouldn't last long.

* * *

To Sara's delight, Clara didn't take a nap. So after a light meal, she and Clara followed Brody back outside, each excited about their little journey.

"Sara," Brody said as they neared her conveyance, "would you rather ride a horse or drive the buggy?"

Sara's eyes lit up, then faded. "And you'll drive Clara around?"

"No, one of my men can do it."

"Well…it has been a long while since I've been on a horse. What do you think, Clara?"

"That's up to you, my dear. I personally loved being on a horse's back when I was your age. I used to ride all over the countryside."

Brody smiled inwardly at seeing Sara's eagerness. "Do you ride sidesaddle or astride?"

Sara thought a moment. "I've never ridden sidesaddle. Will that cause a problem?"

"Not at all." He pointed toward the big stable. "I thought you'd prefer riding, so I took the liberty of having a horse prepared. Red's bringing him now."

Sara turned and looked at the horse being lead out by a cowpoke. To her relief, the animal appeared to be docile.

The impropriety of the situation didn't occur to Sara until she started to step up into the stirrup. She immediately put her foot back down. "Perhaps a sidesaddle would be better."

"Nonsense," Brody said. "Red, help Mrs. Riggs into the buggy."

Red let the horse's reins fall to the ground then went to attend to Clara.

"If you have never ridden sidesaddle, Sara, you'll feel like you're going to fall," Brody informed her.

"Maybe I shouldn't do this."

In one easy move, Brody lifted her up and onto the saddle. "Now put your legs down and I'll adjust the stirrups."

Since no one seemed to care about her skirt being hiked up to the point of showing her ankles, Sara decided not to make an issue of it. Besides, she truly did want to go riding.

"Ol' Buster will give you a good ride," Brody assured her. "He's real easy to rein."

With Red driving the buggy and Brody saddled up, they were ready to go.

By the time they'd viewed some of the cattle and a parcel of the land Brody owned, Sara's legs were feeling the strain. Being in a saddle that straddled the horse's broad back wasn't something she made a daily habit of. In truth, she hadn't ridden since she was thirteen, when her papa had decided that a buggy was more befitting a lady.

Not wanting to be a bother, Sara said nothing of her discomfort, though the pleasure of being lifted down by a pair of strong arms and placed in the buggy was indeed tempting. Or had it been the thought of being pressed against a hard chest that had set her pulse racing earlier?

By the time they returned to the homestead, Sara's discomfort had turned into pure agony. She couldn't even pull her feet from the stirrups. Even after Brody had dismounted his horse, Red and Clara had already climbed from the buggy and Red was unhitching her horse from the conveyance, Sara still hadn't moved.

Brody came up alongside and asked, "Have you forgotten how to dismount?" He chuckled. "All you have to do is hold on to the pommel and swing you leg over—"

"Don't touch me. I can't move."

"What?"

"I said I can't move. I'll never be able to walk again."

Brody finally understood her problem. How could he have been so blind as to not realize how her legs would ache after not being on a horse for so long? He gently took her feet out of the stirrups.

"Be careful!" Sara groaned. "I think my legs are permanently bent."

Brody shook his head and wisely maintained a sober face. "You'll be walking in no time." Nevertheless, he gently lifted her off the horse then placed an arm beneath her knees to make her more comfortable.

"Do you think you can stand?" he asked, still holding her safely in his arms.

"No."

"Poor Sara," Clara sympathized. "You should have said something earlier."

Sara nodded her agreement, but it was doubtful Clara had seen it. Brody was already carrying her to the house.

"Kapata," Brody called as soon as they were inside.

Sara would have sworn the Indian woman had appeared out of nowhere.

Not breaking stride, Brody spoke to housekeeper in some foreign language that Sara didn't understand. He continued on to the bedroom she'd been given.

"Kapata has a liniment that will have you up and around in no time," he informed Sara as he placed her on the bed.

Sara caught a glimpse of Clara waddling right behind him.

"Clara, while Kapata is taking care of Sara, why don't I show you the old cabin that was built many years ago?"

Clara patted Sara's head. "Do you think you'll be all right, sweetie?"

"I'll be fine." Sara wanted to go with them. For a brief moment, she resented Brody spending so much time with Clara.

Brody and Clara left and Kapata came into the room holding a jar of something.

By late afternoon, and a short nap, Sara felt like a new person. Though her legs were still a little sore, the salve Kapata had rubbed on them had worked miracles.

That evening, after a wonderful supper, the threesome moved onto the porch and rocking chairs. They all rocked contentedly and while Brody smoked his cigar, they discussed the multitude of stars in the sky. Later, Clara entertained them with stories of her past.

When Clara stood, ready for bed, Sara rose from her chair, ready to follow. Because Clara's hearing was a bit impaired, she didn't hear Brody softly say, "Why are you afraid to be alone with me, mouse?"

Sara stopped dead in the doorway and turned.

"Are you coming, dear?" Clara called from inside.

"In a minute," Sara called back.

"Don't take long."

"I won't." Sara stepped back onto the porch, staring at Brody, still not believing what she'd heard. "I'm not afraid to be alone with you, Brody. As I've said before, I have a reputation to protect."

"Are you sure that's the reason?"

The candlelight from inside didn't reach the porch, and she could barely see his outline against the dark sky. He'd moved closer. "Why did you call me mouse?"

"It seemed fitting." He trailed his finger down her cheek.

"My father and brother used to call me that."

"Really? What a coincidence. Did you enjoy your day?"

His low voice reminded her of silk. Soft and very appealing. A slight breeze kicked up, sending the heady scent of night jasmine through the air. "Yes." She could feel his nearness, smell that special scent that was exclusively his. She should go in. Clara was waiting.

"Do your legs feel better?"

"My what?"

"From the horseback ride."

"Oh, yes. Much better." He casually leaned against the doorjamb, but there was nothing casual about the way her blood pounded through her veins.

"Are we still friends?"

"I…of course. Brody, not that it matters…I mean, I like the way we've worked things out, but considering your reputation, why is it you're not attracted to me?"

"I never said I wasn't."

Brody backed away then pulled a cigar from his pocket and lit it, leaving Sara to wonder if the conversation had just ended.

"You are a very beautiful and appealing woman." He blew a couple of perfect smoke rings. "But I'll leave you alone. I might get carried away and I don't want to do anything that might jeopardize our friendship. It's been too hard to come by and I'd miss it."

"Oh."

"But should you ever want to change our relationship, I'd be more than happy to oblige. I can assure you, you'd have a smile on your face come morning.''

Sara cleared her throat. He had just invited her to share his bed!

"Only minutes ago I started to kiss you good-night, but I didn't want to chase you off.''

"Surely one little kiss wouldn't hurt?''

He leaned closer.

Her feet where glued to the floor.

"I'm not talking about a quick kiss on the cheek. Good night, mouse.'' He walked past her and into the house.

The pit of Sara's stomach had hit bottom. Again she had waited for a kiss, only to left wanting.

"Sara, are you coming to bed?" Clara called.

Sara took several deep breaths, trying to compose herself. Fortunately the lanterns had been dimmed and Clara wouldn't be able to see Sara's flushed face.

After going to bed, Sara's desire didn't subside as it had on previous occasions. She couldn't sleep knowing Brody was nearby. More than once she fantasized that it was his hands traveling over her body. Thank heavens she and Clara had been given separate rooms.

The sky had changed from indigo blue to gray by the time Sara's eyelids grew heavy.

"Wake up, girl. Are you planning to sleep all day?"

It took several moments for Clara's words to penetrate Sara's deep sleep. "What time is it?" she asked, rubbing her eyes.

"It's nearing ten. Do you normally sleep this late?"

Sara shook her head and rolled onto her side. Clara stood beside the bed, fully dressed and with an expression that indicated to Sara that she'd been waiting for some time. "Have you had breakfast?"

"Nearly four hours ago. Brody has already shown me all the outbuildings."

"Outbuildings?"

"The tannery, blacksmith's area, drying shed…"

"What's a drying shed?" Sara stood and stretched. Surprisingly, she felt quite refreshed.

"You know, where they dry meat and that sort of thing. He could live here nicely and never see another soul. There's even a garden for vegetables, herbs plus flowers. Kapata takes care of those. I'm beginning to think there's nothing the woman can't do."

"Is she Brody's mistress?"

Clara cast a keen eye on her young friend before going over and helping her dress. "Did I hear a note of jealousy from the very same person who claimed she and Brody had become good friends, nothing more?"

"Of course not. I'm simply making conversation."

"I see. Then there's no need to discuss so delicate a matter."

Sara ground her teeth. Clara loved to gossip. Why did she choose now to remain silent?

When they walked in to the great room, the table had been set with all sorts of bowls filled with delicious-looking food.

"Are you hungry?" Brody asked.

"Ravenous."

"I thought you might be, so I had Kapata help me rustle up some food. It's been hours since Clara and I ate. I thought she'd also be feeling a bit hungry. I know I am."

No invitations were needed. They all took a seat around the table.

"These are tortillas," he informed the women as he picked up one of the flat breads. "You take a spoonful of food from a bowl—" he demonstrated with some fried potatoes "—and anything from other bowls that hits your fancy." He added fried eggs then tomatoes and onions. "Tuck in each end so nothing will fall out, then roll it up and take a bite." He smiled as he chewed. "It's a Mexican dish I learned when I was in Mexico. Mighty good."

The women followed suit.

"This is marvelous," Clara exclaimed.

Brody watched Sara wolf down her food then reach for another tortilla. "And what do you think, Sara?"

"Delicious. Are you saying you cooked all this?"

"That's right, but with Kapata's help."

Sara sprinkled cheese on the strips of chicken. Brody never ceased to amaze her. She would never have pictured him cooking anything, especially not a feast like this. "Perhaps you'll teach me how to prepare it." She took another big bite, savoring the taste as she chewed.

"I'd be happy to. I'm sure there are a lot of other things I could teach you as well."

Sara didn't dare look at him. Was he referring to what she thought he was referring to? Right in front of Clara? Surely he was toying with her again. The man had no scruples.

"Unfortunately," Brody added after he finished the last of his food, "you won't be here long enough on this visit. We'll have to do it next time."

"There won't be a next time." Sara nervously placed her napkin on the table, shoved her chair back and looked at Clara. "We really should be heading back to town."

"So soon?" Clara protested, making her disappointment obvious. "Brody waited until you woke to show us his stable."

"We do have a long drive ahead. You should have awakened me sooner."

"But you have to see the stable." Brody stood and pulled Clara's chair back for her.

"He has a surprise." Clara placed her hand over her mouth.

"Shame on you, Clara," Brody teased. "Now the secret is out."

"Me and my mouth. Well," Clara said as she went out the front door, her arm tucked around Brody's, "it won't be the first time I should have kept my mouth shut." She looked up at Brody adoringly.

Left with no choice, Sara followed. "What sort of surprise?" she called after them. The pair continued on toward the stable as if she hadn't even spoken.

"All right," Sara conceded, "but we can't spend much time admiring horses!" Still they ignored her. Her temper had started to rise.

When they reached their destination, Sara stopped at the entrance, smelling the pleasing odors of saddle soap, leather and freshly spread straw in the stalls. The stable was large and meticulously clean. But she was in no mood to appreciate it. As Brody and Clara continued down the center between the stalls, he pointed out various horses and continued a nonstop orientation on his breeding stock and his plans for the future.

"Stop!" Sara yelled out. Clara and Brody stopped and turned. Sara realized her blunder when the horses moved nervously in their stalls and snorted their protest at the unexpected loudness. Nevertheless, she wasn't about to apologize. "You said you have a surprise, Brody. Where is it? As I have already said, Clara and I need to be on our way."

"It's down at the end," Brody replied patiently. "Come along and I'll show you."

Sara gritted her teeth. How dare he talk to her as if she were a naughty child!

Brody stopped and the prettiest paint she had ever laid eyes on stuck her head out of the stall to greet her visitor. Sara reluctantly moved forward. When she reached Brody's side, the mare moved to the back of the stall.

"Sara, isn't she a beauty?" Clara asked.

Sara couldn't take her eyes off the mare. The black-and-white coloring brought out her perfect features and her long mane lay in ripples across her powerful neck.

"Buckets, meet your new owner."

It took a moment for Brody's words to penetrate. "What?"

"This is the surprise. The mare is yours. It's a gift for being a guest at my ranch."

"But...I could never accept such a gift." Sara couldn't remember ever wanting anything as badly as she wanted the beautiful horse.

"But, Sara," Clara spouted, "Brody bought the mare especially for you."

"Of course she's feisty and may be too much for you, especially after your being so uncomfortable yesterday."

"I can't take her," Sara persisted. *But if Clara thought it was all right...*

Brody winked at Clara. "Then I guess I'll just have to sell her."

Sara gasped. "You can't do that."

"I have no use for the mare. It was just a friendly gesture. When I saw her I thought she'd be the perfect saddle horse for you."

"You did?"

"Just for the heck of it, why don't I saddle her up and you can take her for a ride around the corral?"

"We really should be going."

Brody heard the lack of haste in her voice. "You're right. I won't detain you any longer. Besides, you're still too sore from yesterday's ride."

"I'm not that sore," Sara quickly assured him. "Are you really going to sell her?"

"I have my own saddle horses. Buckets needs someone to exercise her."

"Who named her Buckets?"

"The previous owner. He told me she got her name because when her water bucket became empty, she'd pick it up and carry it to him. I'm told she does other tricks as well."

"That's a terrible name." Sara grinned. "But I think I like it."

"So do I." Not for a moment had Brody failed to notice how Sara's anger had subsided.

"Why does she stand in the back of her stall?"

"You're a stranger."

"If I rode her a little every day, we could get used to each other. I'll accept your gift. I couldn't bear knowing she'd been sold," she lied. Actually owning such a beautiful animal already had her feeling giggly inside.

"Then it's done." He took hold of Clara's arm. "As Sara said, you really need to be on your way."

"But what about Buckets?" Sara asked, still standing in front of the stall.

"I'll keep her here. I'd rather be near when you start riding her. Like I said, she's a bit frisky." He walked away, taking Clara with him.

Sara hurried forward. "How am I suppose to learn when she's here and I'm in town?"

Brody stopped, pretending to assess the situation. "Pick a week when Clara can be available and come back. By the end of the week you'll be riding Buckets across fields."

"But..."

"I have nothing planned for next week," Clara said. "Seven days here would be an absolute delight."

"Then next week it shall be." Brody started walking again.

"Can we please discuss this?" Sara demanded.

Brody waited for her to catch up to him.

"I have a company to take care of," Sara reminded them. "I can't just take off for a week."

Brody frowned. "If I can, you can."

Sara glared at the tall, rugged man. Had he planned all this from the beginning? No, she was just being overly suspicious. Buckets nickered. She looked back at her gift. Buckets's big, round eyes ended all arguments. "All right, I'll make arrangements."

All during the ride home, Sara wondered if she wouldn't have been smarter to just let Brody sell the horse. But she just couldn't take the chance he really might do it, and she wanted that mare.

Why did her plans always seem to go awry? Now she'd have to wait until next week to tell Brady she never wanted to see him again.

Chapter Thirteen

Due to Brody and Clara's insistence, a week later Brody escorted the ladies on their return to the ranch. A sidesaddle lay in the back of the buggy with the various pieces of luggage. Sara had decided that when she and Buckets made their debut on the streets of Leavenworth, it would be done in a style acceptable even to the self-appointed town aristocrats.

"I want you to know that I've only returned to prove I can ride Buckets," Sara called to Brody, seated atop a prancing gray gelding. "Once that's accomplished I see no reason to delay our stay."

"I agree."

Sara opened her mouth ready to defend her case, but Brody's reply wasn't what she'd expected. This past week had been spent rebuilding her determination to end their relationship. A little pleasure wasn't worth the heartache. She'd even rehearsed rebuttals for when he'd try talking her out of it. But he'd agreed. Had he lost interest in her during the past week?

When her bags were delivered to her room Sara didn't bother to unpack. If everything went smoothly, she'd be heading straight home. If Clara wanted to stay, Brody could return her to town.

A few minutes later, Sara headed for the stable, with Brody and Clara following close behind. But on the way, Sara spied Buckets saddled and tethered inside a corral. It had to be Brody's doings. It was eerie the way he somehow always managed to second-guess her. Could it possibly be that he was just as eager to see her leave early?

Sara and Brody entered the small corral and Clara gingerly moved off to the side where she could look through the fence rails. Sara could hardly wait to show off her expertise. Unbeknownst to the others, she'd taken private lessons on riding sidesaddle.

As they neared Buckets, the mare twitched her withers and moved her rump to the side, allowing a clear view of the man and woman approaching. The closer they came, the more the mare backed away until she had reached the end of the reins.

Brody took Sara's arm and brought her to a halt. ''I don't think we should go any closer. Something's wrong.''

''Just help me mount her, Brody,'' Sara said impatiently. ''I assure you everything will be fine.''

"I don't think so. She's never rolled her eyes or laid her ears back before."

"Horses just do that." But when Sara took a step forward, the mare lunged at her, her big teeth snapping. Brody reached out and grabbed Sara away just in time to keep from being bit.

Even Sara could see how stiff-legged the paint now stood.

"Did you give me a horse that isn't broken?" Sara asked suspiciously.

"Not at all. I've ridden her all over and haven't had a bit of trouble. Maybe it's the perfume you're wearing."

Sara buried her hands in the folds of her lemon-yellow dress. "Or maybe it's the bright color of my gown?"

Brody shrugged his shoulders.

"Wait here. I'll go change."

As soon as Sara walked out the gate, the mare relaxed.

Brody stroked the shiny neck. "You're not going to make this easy, are you? Good. I would have been disappointed if you did." The moment he had seen the mare being unloaded from a paddle wheeler a couple of weeks ago, he knew he had to have her. Physically, the three-year-old was flawless. He considered her high-spirited disposition an added asset. Yet she was gentle and easily reined, as long as he was in the saddle.

"Where did Sara go?" Clara called.

"To change clothes. She thinks the color of her dress may have spooked the horse."

Sara returned wearing a simple white blouse and navy-blue skirt with wide pockets. Again when she approached, the mare shied away. "Apparently the color had nothing to do with this." She turned to Brody. "Give me a foot up and let's see if she behaves herself."

"Very well, but I don't think it's a good idea."

"Well, we can't just stand here. Let's at least try."

Instead of cupping his hands, Brody raised her up by the waist. The minute she touched the saddle, Buckets bucked, sending Sara off into midair. Fortunately, Brody caught her in his arms.

Brody looked down at her and chucked. "So much for your idea."

"You can let me down now."

Brody put her on her feet. "What? No thank you?"

"Thank you," Sara mumbled.

"Well, I guess that's a start."

Clara stepped up on a low fence rail so she could be heard. "Maybe Buckets just doesn't like women."

Brody scratched the back of his head. "You know, now that I think about it, the man I bought her from said Buckets used to be his wife's horse. Maybe she mistreated the mare. It would certainly explain her behavior." He took Sara's arm and led her out of the corral. "Let me think on it."

Sara returned to her room and glared at her luggage. Should she just forget about Buckets? She started unpacking.

After supper, Sara slipped out of the house and headed for the stable. She'd only been there less than fifteen minutes when someone entered behind her.

"What are you doing out here all alone? I thought you'd gone to bed." She looked quite comfortable perched on top of a bale of hay.

"Trying to get Buckets used to me."

"How long have you been here?"

"Not long. I couldn't get Buckets's dislike for me out of my head. Most horses like me."

"Runaway does. You know I can always find you a different horse. You don't have to put up with this one's temperament."

"No," Sara said slowly. "She just needs to know we can be friends and that I don't give up easily."

Brody smiled. Sara had a way with words that could easily apply to him. "You sure?"

Sara nodded.

"In that case, I have an idea."

Sara jumped to her feet. "I know you know a lot about horses," she said excitedly, "but do you honestly think you can get her to trust me?"

"We can certainly give it a try." He walked over and rubbed Buckets's velvety nose.

Sara joined him and Buckets moved to the far end of the stall. "She definitely doesn't like me."

"Don't wear that perfume tomorrow. We'll see if that has anything to do with it. I know it certainly has an effect on me." He led her away. "Come along. Nothing can be done tonight."

Sara mulled over his comment about her perfume having an effect on him. She shivered as they walked out into the open.

"You cold?" Brody asked.

"There is a bit of a nip in the air tonight."

"Here, let me keep you warm." Brody placed his big arm around her slender shoulders. "You'll have to admit that other than the chill, it's a fine night. The full moon is lighting our path all the way to the house."

Sara hardly heard a word he said. Walking beside him had definitely warmed her body. She thought to pull away, but didn't.

"Don't you agree?"

"Oh, yes. Absolutely." Was he still discussing the moon?

They walked in silence, Sara drinking in her moment of happiness.

"Did you hear that?"

"What?" Brody asked.

"The howling."

"There are nights when the coyotes are so noisy you wish they'd shut up."

Sara pulled away from him but continued walking. "Brody, from some of the things you've said I've got-

ten the impression that you'd rather Clara and I didn't
stay the week.''

''It was my impression that you're the one eager to
leave. I simply agreed.''

Sara's relief surprised her. However, it was one
thing for her to want to leave and an different matter
if *he* wanted her to go.

''Just what is it that makes you so uncomfortable.
Is it the ranch?''

''Oh, no. It's wonderful here.''

''Then it must be me.''

Sara felt like an animal that had just been caught in
a trap. ''You are a bit unsettling.''

They reached the house. Sara stepped up onto the
porch, her footsteps sounding loud in the night's still-
ness.

''Am I? As a friend or a possible lover?''

Sara clutched the porch rail. ''I—I only think of you
as a friend.''

''You're lying.'' He moved past her to the door.
''It's what you want to believe. Your problem with
me is that I make you aware of your desires. You're
every bit as aware of me as I am of you, and we both
know we can never be *just* friends. Good night, Sara.''

After he'd left, Sara managed to catch her breath.
From the moment she'd first laid eyes on him her life
had become a turmoil. Now he was even telling her
she wanted him. It galled her that he found it so easy

to look into her mind, especially when what he'd said had been true. How did he remain unaffected?

She hurried into the house and went directly to her room. She'd show him he didn't know her as well as he thought. He could go on talking, but she would no longer let it affect on her. The time had come for someone to tell him no and mean it.

Sara rose early the following morning, but Brody had already had his breakfast and was sipping coffee by the time she entered the great room.

"Good morning," he greeted.

"It is indeed a beautiful morning," she replied in a singsong voice, even though she'd spent almost the entire night awake. As soon as she sat down, Kapata brought a plate of eggs, pork chops, gravy and biscuits and placed it in front of her.

"I take it you had a good night's sleep."

"I slept like a baby," Sara fibbed.

"I didn't."

"Oh?"

"I kept thinking about how it would have turned out if I'd carried you to my bed last night."

Sara nervously glanced about to see if anyone had heard him. "I would never have allowed it." Luckily, Clara apparently hadn't left her room yet.

"Come, come, Sara, I'm not some young sop who knows nothing of what he's doing. I know when a woman wants to be made love to."

"You know nothing." Sara wanted to crawl under the table. "This is not a proper subject for discussion," she whispered.

His lips spread into a devilish grin. "Why not?"

"Please, keep your voice down. Someone might hear you."

"Don't tell me you're one of those prudes who believes sex should only be discussed in the privacy of the bedroom."

"I don't think it's proper to discuss it period." She cut into the juicy pork chop.

Brody leaned back in his chair and studied her. "Well, I'll be. I suppose if we were married it would be acceptable."

Sara swallowed. "Gentlemen and ladies do not speak of such matters, married or not."

"And who told you that?"

"I refuse to discuss it."

"But we are discussing it.

Sara glared at him.

"And I have news for you. Sex is talked about openly by most people. That includes females and males. Of course there are exceptions to everything. Some spouses only make love in the dark and never see each other naked. I personally believe that most men haven't an inkling as to what is expected of them other than the satisfaction of their needs and begetting children."

"You could show a little respect by not speaking

of such things, or has respect vanished after last night's speech?''

"You belittle yourself, my dear. I wonder if your attitude is due to being abused by Malcolm Speck?''

Sara dropped her fork onto her plate.

Brody shoved his chair back and stood. "I want to try something today with Buckets. When you're finished eating, I'll meet you at the same corral we used yesterday." Brody left.

"Wait just one minute!''

"Good morning everyone," Clara said as she waltzed into the room. "Is something wrong?" she inquired. "You look upset."

"No, nothing is wrong. He has an idea about Buckets he wants to try out." Sara's appetite had vanished. How had Brody known about Malcolm? She wanted answers, and she wanted them now! She itched to find out, but Clara had a suspicious nature. So, she chose to wait fifteen minutes before going to search for the big man.

Sara didn't have to look far. She found Brody waiting with Buckets in the corral. She opened the gate and marched in.

"You forgot to close the gate behind you."

Sara sneered. "I don't give a hang about the gate."

"As you can see, I've brought out a chair and I've placed your saddle beside it."

"I don't care about the chair either," Sara snapped at him. She stopped in front of him, wishing they were on an even level. He stood so much taller, she always had to tilt her head back and look up. "You deliberately mentioned Malcolm's name knowing good and well I wouldn't let it drop there. Now I want to know what he told you."

Brody moved forward, forcing her to move back. The back of her knees hit the wooden chair and buckled, making her flop down on the seat. She started to rise, only to be shoved back down.

"If you'll notice, there's no rope around Buckets's neck. She's free to move about as she pleases."

"I don't want to talk about... You are the most insufferable man I've—"

"I'm going to leave the two of you alone in the corral."

Again she tried to stand and again she was pushed back down.

"If you shove me one more time, I'm going to—"

"Then don't stand and listen to what I'm telling you. Besides, you're starting to spook your horse."

His calm demeanor was driving her mad. "I want to talk about Malcolm. Not Buckets." She started to stand again then thought better of it. Her bottom was getting sore from being plopped down on the hard oak seat.

"Malcolm told me nothing. I've never met the man." Brody sauntered toward the open gate.

Sara pulled off a shoe and hurled it at him. "Ha," she laughed when it struck him in the back. "If you think I'm going to sit here, you have another think coming. I'll be gone from this place within five minutes if you don't tell me how you knew about Malcolm!''

Brody picked up the shoe and continued on, closing the gate behind him. "It's quite simple," he said, looking over the fence rail. "I had you investigated a week after you settled into your new building. I've always made a point of knowing about my competition, especially when she has little difficulty taking business away from her competitors.''

His tone of voice was cold and his words clipped, leaving Sara shocked, appalled and embarrassed, in exactly that order. How dare he pry into her personal life? Obviously he even knew of her affair with Malcolm. How foolish she'd been to think she could move to Leavenworth and leave that part of her life behind. He probably considered her a tease by not letting him bed her, especially after having an affair with another man.

"Here's what I want you to do, Sara. I want you to sit still, but if you do move, do it slowly. I want you to talk to Buckets, but keep it gentle.''

Sara's humiliation kept her from looking at him. "And what is the purpose of this?'' she asked quietly, her eyes glued on the mare standing in the far corner.

"I want her to get used to you and hopefully come to you of her own accord. Let her think that the only way she'll be taken for a ride will be with you on her back.''

"All right.'' The words barely escaped her lips. She wanted to return to Leavenworth and bury herself in her work, but she wouldn't. Pride would not allow her to let Brody know the effect his words had had on her. How many others had he shared his information with?

It took all the mettle Sara could muster just to remain seated and talk soothingly to the beautiful black-and-white paint.

Brody left with her shoe in hand.

Sara remembered him once saying that she had no idea as to how ruthless he could be if he wanted something bad enough. She had just had a small taste of it.

An hour later Brody returned. Buckets had moved but still kept her distance from Sara.

"Do you still think it's going to work?'' Sara asked.

"I don't know, but if it does, it's going to take some time. It's getting hot, so why don't you go in the house and we'll give it another try later this afternoon, then again in the morning.'' He tossed her shoe to her.

"I am thirsty,'' she admitted.

Sara slipped her shoe on and headed for the gate that Brody held open. She walked out, making sure she wasn't close enough to brush against him, then stopped.

"Now I know why you called me mouse.''

Brody made no reply.

"Why didn't you inform me of your investigation,

then? No, don't bother answering. You were having fun at my expense. Who have you shared the information with? The first time we danced, you said the townswomen considered me a woman of loose morals. Was it because of what you had told them?''

Brody's green eyes darkened. "I've spoken to no one about the matter. What I learned had nothing to do with freighting."

"And just what did you learn?"

"That your family had been honest, upstanding people."

Sara wanted to scream. "There had to be more or you wouldn't know about Malcolm."

"I know that you and Speck were lovers and that he walked out on you with half your money. I didn't consider that anyone's business, either."

"Nor was it any of yours. But since you're so nosy, you need to get a few of your facts straight. The only money he left with was what I gave him to get rid of him. And yes, we had a short affair, so I know what it's like to be with a man."

"But you haven't been with me."

Sara gave him a killing look. "I have news for you. All men are alike."

"Now there's where you're wrong."

"While I'm confessing all, is there anything else you would like to know? I'd rather provide the information myself than have you hear it from other sources."

"I'm not going to apologize for having you investigated. You've become liked and respected in the business and community. I have no intention of changing that."

"How patronizing of you." She hauled off and socked him in the stomach, hard enough to hear air rush out his mouth. At least she'd received an ounce of satisfaction upon seeing his shocked expression. "It's a wonder I'm good enough to take to your bed. As a matter of fact, I'm surprised you haven't tried using your scraps of information to get me to there."

"I'd be lying if I said I didn't think of it, but it didn't serve my purpose."

She turned in circles, kicking at the ground. "You are below low."

She let go with another blow. "You think you can just—"

Sara started to sock him again, but this time he had anticipated it. He grabbed her wrist and twisted it behind her back. "You would never have known about it, my dear, if I hadn't told you."

Sara leaned over and bit his hand. The minute he released his hold she took off running. "My, oh my," she heard him say. "She does have a temper."

He sounded amused rather than apologetic. Since Brody apparently had no intention of pursuing her, Sara slowed to a fast walk.

For the past hour she had sat conjuring up every conceivable thing he might have done with his information about Malcolm, only to find out he'd told no one, that is if she could believe him.

The man had no conscience.

Later that afternoon, Sara returned to her chair in the corral. But instead of thinking about Brody, she concentrated on Buckets. She realized that though she hated to admit it, Brody could be right about his approach to her problem with the mare. It made sense. If the past owner's wife had mistreated Buckets as Brody suspected, it was up to her to show the mare that all women were not alike.

Sara lay on her bed that night, eyes wide-open. No wonder she couldn't sleep. She'd gone to her room way too early, just to avoid Brody. She flopped onto her back. Sleep was impossible. She jumped off the bed, went to the door and slowly opened it. The house was silent.

Sara returned to the bed, yanked off a quilt and wrapped it around herself. Though the nights had turned chilly, she felt a need for fresh air. She left her room and silently tiptoed though the house and onto the front porch. After settling into one of the big rockers, she inhaled deeply, letting the crisp air fill her lungs.

"So you couldn't sleep, either?"

Sara jumped to her bare feet. The moon offered enough light to see Brody standing in the doorway. "How did you know I was out here?"

"You passed right by me in the parlor."

"You could have had the decency to have a lantern turned up."

Brody smiled.

Wearing only her nightdress, Sara clutched the quilt tighter around her. "I'd like you to leave. I came out here because I wanted to be alone."

"I, on the other hand, wanted to be kissed goodnight." He stepped onto the porch.

"What?" Sara backed away, glancing behind her. There was no place to go. He blocked the door. "Brody—" He moved toward her.

"I should have taken my good-night kiss on your last visit."

"Brody, I really think you were right about it interfering with our friendship. Now if you'll—"

"Friendship, perhaps, lovers, no."

"We're not lovers," she said angrily. Wrapped up like a cocoon she could do nothing.

"Not yet." Grasping the folds of the quilt, he gently drew her to him. He tugged at her bottom lip with his teeth and felt her tremble with expectancy. "Ever since I kissed you the night of the ball, I've wanted to taste your sweetness again." His lips brushed against hers as he spoke.

"Don't do this," Sara pleaded, her body already tense. How long had she waited for his kiss?

His mouth hungrily covered hers, and the whole world began to reel. Her pulse raced as his kiss deepened, his tongue exploring the inner recesses...

draining all resistance as his lips moved over hers, devouring the softness.

"Let me make your dreams come true, Sara."

What had happened to her determination to resist him?

"I don't think I can stop," he whispered before burying his face in the curve of her neck. "I want to love you all night and see the smile on your face come morning."

Sara felt dampness between her legs as she pressed against him, then leaned her head back so he could suck where her pulse beat. She was shocked at her own eager response. Lord help her, she wanted to feel their bodies crushed together. Again his lips captured hers, her breast tightening as his hand slid under the quilt.

"Tell me to stop," he whispered before he smothered his words with her mouth.

She couldn't nor did she try to stop the moan of pleasure as he slowly, maddeningly, brushed his thumb over her hardened nipple. But somehow she managed to gather all her strength and pull away, letting the quilt fall to the floor. "Keep your hands off me!"

Brody moved back to the door. "You're probably right to end it. I want you, Sara. I want you in my bed. I want to memorize every curve of your body. I want to hear you scream with desire as I take you to heights you've never known. But not this way."

"What do you mean?" Unlike her, he seemed totally unaffected by their kiss.

"I don't want you claiming I seduced you. Come morning you would have convinced yourself it was all wrong, and later throw it in my face by saying it was all my fault."

Sara's breathing was slowly returning to normal. "You just can't handle a woman not succumbing to your advances. What would you have expected next? For me to go to your room and ask you to make love to me?"

"Then we'd both know it's something you chose, not something I talked you into. Too bad, you would have loved it."

Sara was furious. "Well, don't hold your breath or you'll die, which would be just fine with me. I'll never grovel at you feet."

Brody chuckled. "I never considered it groveling. I consider lovemaking a pleasure shared by two."

Sara's mouth was still hanging open when he disappeared into the house. First thing in the morning she'd leave. Though she'd never admit it to another soul, he was too persuasive. Even now she wanted him to take her back in his arms.

He had been right. She was running away from something that had no future, only misery. It had been a long time since she'd made love and it was going to be a lot longer. She had thought she could spend the rest of her life being celibate, but Brody had proven that wrong. Nevertheless, the next man she gave herself to would be offering a wedding ring.

At daybreak Sara left the house. Her bags had already been packed. All she needed to do was hook her horse up to the buggy. Once that had been accomplished all she'd need to return for was her luggage and Clara.

Fifteen minutes later, Sara returned to her room. The blacksmith had told her that a split in the axle had been discovered. That was his reason for all the wheels having been removed from her buggy.

An hour later, she openly accused Brody of keeping her a prisoner.

"Would you have wanted me to let you return with a cracked axle?"

The innocent look on his face made Sara want to hit him.

"He's right, Sara," Clara said. "We could have been killed. And why would he want to deliberately do such a thing?"

"He wants…" Sara hesitated.

Brody raised a dark brow and waited. "I want what?"

"He wants what, dear?" Clara repeated.

"I'm probably too worried over Buckets to think straight." Why, of all mornings, had Clara chosen to get up early?

For the next three days, Sara faithfully sat twice a day in the corral, most of the time cooing soothing words to her horse. The ranch hands had started taking an interest and collected at the fence, placing wagers as to who would win out. The horse or the beautiful lady.

The rest of the time Sara remained at Clara's side, never giving Brody an opportunity to catch her alone, except when she sat with Buckets. But when he never made an appearance, she began to wonder if she was the one keeping him at arm's length or if it was the other way around.

However, Brody made sure she was reminded of his presence. There were the devilish, knowing smiles and the subtle comments that eluded Clara. But mostly it was his self-confidence that kept her wondering what he would be like in bed.

It all combined to give her the worst nights she'd ever experienced. She could see him clearly, even with her eyes closed.

Chapter Fourteen

Sara smiled broadly as she and Clara left the tannery. The divided skirt she'd asked the tanner to make two weeks ago had turned out even better than she'd hoped for. He'd even made a vest to go with it.

Sara placed the items over her arm as she and Clara continued their daily walk.

"What a shame," Clara declared as she opened her umbrella to block the sun.

"Why did you say that?"

The two women reached down and hiked up their skirts to keep as little dirt as possible from collecting.

"We've already been here five days, and in just two more we'll be departing."

"Assuming the buggy is ready by then."

"Brody assured me it would be. I have grown quite fond of this place and shall miss it when we've left."

Sara made no comment. The sooner they were gone the happier she'd be.

"Sara, dear," Clara said, "are you not feeling well?"

"I feel fine. Why do you ask?"

Sara kept an eye out for the rooster that had been waiting for them the last two days. The obnoxious bird had talons that would make any fighting cock proud, and he seemed determined to try them out on her.

"Well, there was that little episode when you accused Brody of keeping us prisoners, plus you're simply not your lively self. And I do declare you're getting bags under your eyes. You're much too young for that sort of thing."

"I must admit, I haven't been sleeping well."

"Then you should have Kapata fix you a cup of chamomile tea before going to bed."

"Look over there." Sara pointed toward a corral where dust kept shooting into the air.

"I do believe the men are breaking wild horses," Clara said excitedly. "I haven't seen that since leaving Kentucky. Let's go over and watch."

They reached the fence just in time to see Brody dismount a roan he'd broken.

"That's it for the day, boys," he told the other men. He crawled up and over the fence on the other side.

"Oh," Clara sighed, "we're too late."

"He's gotta get back to that sweet little lady stayin' in his house," one of the men teased—loud enough for Brody to hear.

"Aw," a towheaded man said, "you're just jealous."

"You're damn right I am."

They all laughed.

"They haven't seen us, Clara," Sara said. "I feel almost guilty for having eavesdropped. Let's leave before they find out we're here."

"They said nothing wrong," Clara protested.

"I know, but they wouldn't have made those remarks had they known we were here. Hopefully we can slip away before being noticed."

As she was about to turn away, the problem solved itself. The men left the corral and headed toward the bunkhouse, which was also in the opposite direction. Sara released a sigh. Clara had been right, there really wasn't a good reason for feeling guilty. Nevertheless, she felt a lot better knowing their presence hadn't been detected.

The ladies decided to return to the house. They hadn't gone far when Sara caught sight of Brody leaning over with his head under a water pump. He had removed his shirt, and as he rinsed his face and hair, the muscles across his back and arms rippled. He raised up and shook his head, sending rivulets of water flying in every direction.

Sara quickened her steps, not wanting Clara or Brody to know what she had witnessed. But the scene had been branded in her mind. She had never seen such a perfect body. The sudden urge to touch and run her hands over him caused her to stumble. Somehow she managed to catch herself before falling.

"Are you all right, dear?" Clara asked worriedly.

"Yes. I had been thinking about Buckets and not paying attention to the path."

"If you ask me, I think you're coming down with something. I'm going to have a talk with Brody about you sitting out in the corral with that mare for so long. It's not healthy."

"But I want to do it. I'll tell you a little secret if you promise not to tell Brody."

Clara's interest had been piqued. "My lips are sealed."

"Buckets turned and looked at me this morning."

Clara stopped beneath a wide-branched tree, welcoming the shade. "That's the secret?"

"Isn't it wonderful? She even pricked her ears forward."

"Yes, it's wonderful," Clara repeated, already having lost interest. "I think you should let Brody sell the mare and find you a proper horse to ride."

They started walking again.

"Your nose is peeling from being in the sun too long," Clara pointed out.

"If you have to work for something, Clara, it becomes all the more precious to you. That's how I feel about Buckets. At this point, nothing in the world could change my desire for her."

Sara suddenly realized that the same thing applied

to Brody. He had ignited a desire within her the likes of which she had never experienced before. How could she have been so foolish to think that given time, she'd grow immune to his masculinity?

It wasn't going to happen.

The more he stayed away from her the more she wanted him near. Even when they dined, she watched his hands, wishing she could feel them on her body. She watched the way he moved, the stoic way he kept his thoughts from others, the timbre of his voice and how special she felt when she'd turn and catch him watching her.

No, this was not something that would pass. The fire he'd created couldn't be smothered, and he knew it. He was like a puma, settled in the bush and waiting for his prey. She hated him for it.

After leaving Clara at the house, Sara went to the corral to sit with Buckets. There were at least ten men sitting on the top rails, watching. When they talked to one another, they kept they voices low.

The mare stood in the center, and when Sara closed the gate behind her, Buckets didn't move away. She looked up at the cowhands and grinned. Returning her smile, they all nodded their approval.

Sara made a wide circle around the paint then sat quietly in her chair. Buckets had definitely become used to her presence. Slowly Sara raised the sidesaddle and placed it in her lap. "If you would like to go for a ride, I'd be happy to oblige you," she crooned.

An hour and a half later, Sara entered the house, her face beaming as brightly as the sunflowers in the fields.

"You're late," Clara chastised. "We've been waiting supper and I'm famished."

The moment they sat at the table, Kapata began serving the food.

"So Buckets came to you tonight," Brody said before taking a bite of meat.

Sara looked up. "You saw?" she asked, her excitement bubbling over.

"No, I've just come to know you very well. You're elated about something, and the only thing I can think of would be Buckets." Actually, the hands had kept him informed daily of the progress.

Sara leaned forward. "Oh, Brody, it was the most wonderful experience. She put her head down and walked straight to me. I was afraid to move, but she nuzzled my hands for the carrot I had. When I gave it to her, she didn't turn away. She stayed right there. Finally I tried walking slowly around the corral and she actually followed me!"

"Your plan worked, Brody," Clara commented, not at all interested in the conversation.

"Ah, but Sara did all the work."

"I'm so excited I doubt I can eat a thing. Brody, when do you think I can ride her? I was afraid to put the saddle on for fear I might chase her off."

"We'll start working on it tomorrow."

"Do you think it will be all right?"

"We won't know, Sara, until we try. You know what, I think this calls for a celebration."

Clara's eyes lit up.

"I have bourbon and wine, and I have a piano," Brody continued, "but no one ever plays it. If I remember, Clara, can't you play the instrument?"

"I certainly can."

They all rose from the table, their eyes lit up with anticipation and the meal left untouched.

Kapata looked questioningly at Brody. Though Sara didn't understand what Brody told the attractive woman, it had to have had something to do with the party because Kapata clapped her hands with delight. She did understand the word party.

After accepting a glass of bourbon, Clara sat at the piano and began playing a rousing tune. To Sara's delight, ranch hands started sticking their heads through the open window, apparently attracted by the music.

Others moseyed up and in no time a man with a long beard and a fiddle appeared.

"Come in and join us for a drink," Brody said. "We're having a little celebration."

The fiddler moved to the piano and raised the instrument to his chin.

A young ranch hand headed straight for Sara. "I'd be right pleased if you'd be my partner in a set, ma'am."

"It would be my pleasure."

A circle was quickly formed of all the men and Sara. Clara played the music and the fiddler did the calling. Minutes later, Kapata joined in.

This time Sara didn't need dancing instructions. She'd spent many happy hours with her pa and brother at jamborees, square dancing the night away.

While Kapata, Sara and often Clara paired off with one man then another, Brody chose to stand back and watch. He couldn't help but wonder where Clara had come up with such a burst of energy. She also had a strong stomach when it came to downing her liquor.

After the first time Sara had sat in the corral with Buckets, she had forsaken her fancy gowns for plain attire. Tonight she'd worn a white, Gypsy-style blouse with embroidered flowers and a gingham skirt that stopped at the top of her low-heeled shoes. Her silver-blond hair had been parted in the center and pulled straight back into a bun.

Her natural beauty shone like a star, and Brody was well aware that every man in the room wanted her, including him.

He sipped his drink. Never had he waited so long to bed a woman. It reminded him of a chess game, and so far she'd blocked his every move.

With most of the men having to rise before dawn, the party didn't last long, but Sara didn't mind. She, Kapata and Clara were quite exhausted after so much dancing.

When the men had left, Sara collapsed into one of the deep chairs. Clara and Kapata went directly to their quarters.

"Aren't you being a bit daring tonight?" Brody asked before lighting a cigar. "Lately you've been running off to your room."

Sara's mind was still on the evening's fun. "I don't run away. I simply go to my room early to avoid you."

"Clara told me that you haven't been getting much sleep."

Sara squirmed. "I'm not used to the bed. After tonight I'm sure sleep will not be a problem."

"I can help you sleep."

"I doubt that." She glanced at him then quickly looked away. The good Lord had to have been angry with women when he created Brody. Surely he'd been put here for the sole purpose of breaking women's hearts. The devil's temptation.

Though Brody hadn't kissed or touched her, never had she wanted anything as much as she wanted him to take her to his bed. He was so compelling, and his magnetism too potent. How much longer could she go on telling herself she didn't need him?

Sara rose from her chair. It was just the two of them. All she had to do was ask him to make love to her. But it would be tantamount to giving up the fight, and the words just wouldn't come. "Good night," she said softly.

As she passed, Brody reached out and gently drew

her to him. He felt a shiver shoot through her body. Curious, he raised her chin with his finger, forcing her look at him. Desire was written on her face and her beautiful brown eyes mirrored her passion.

"Who are you fighting, Sara? Yourself or me?" He swooped her up in his arms and headed for his bedroom.

Sara couldn't think. Pictures of him without his shirt kept floating in her mind.

"Damned if you aren't the most stubborn woman I've ever known," Brody said with humor. "You want me every bit as much as I want you. Even Adam and Eve enjoyed the fruits of pleasure."

Sara curled up against his hard chest, aware of the strength and warmth of his flesh. Her heart thumped in her ears as he closed the door behind them. Having acknowledged her need for him, she was filled with anticipation. Just being in his arms made her want more. All her past resistance now seemed so pointless.

"You were right all along," Sara admitted, her vitality rising. "It was just a matter of time."

Brody leaned down and kissed her ripe lips before placing her on his bed. Her eyes were clouded and her full lips parted as his kisses followed each piece of clothing he removed. Sara brazenly watched him shed his clothes, mesmerized by the magnificence of his body and eager for him to join her on the bed...until his last piece of clothing fell to the floor. Her gasp was loud enough for him to hear.

"Is something wrong?"

She gulped. Compared to Brody, Malcolm was tiny. "I—I—" Sara didn't know how to say it. "I don't know...I'm not sure I can accommodate you. You're so big." There. She'd said it.

Brody laughed as he lay on the bed facing her. "I promise to be gentle."

She'd become very still, her body stiff as he trailed a finger down her neck and between her tempting breasts. "You're even more beautiful than I imagined."

Her stomach twitched as his hand caressed the flat, satiny skin. He kissed the corners of her lips and was tempted to suckle a pert nipple that beckoned him. Instead, he bent his elbow and rested his head on his hand, enjoying the sight of her unabashed nakedness. Her eyes were closed and an undeniable look of pleasure and expectancy was spread across her fine features. So why did she continue to be so stiff?

Sara cocked an eye open. Seeing he was just staring at her, she opened the other one. "Is something wrong?"

"Didn't you tell me your Mr. Speck made love to you?"

Sara bolted upright into a sitting position. "This isn't exactly the time to be asking such a question, or have you changed your mind about making love to me? I will not beg if that's what you have in mind."

He looked down at his erection. "Does it look to you like I've changed my mind?"

"I haven't inquired about your women friends, so why are you asking about Malcolm?"

"Is he the only man you've ever made love to?"

"Oh! I've had enough of this cross-examination." She started to climb off the bed, only to be pulled back down.

"I've planned for this moment too damn long to let you run away."

Again she tried to bound off the bed. This time he pulled her back down and pinned her with his body. "I should have known that when you're involved, nothing goes as expected."

"Get off of me or I'll scream and awaken everyone in the house including your Indian lover."

Sara was mortified when he broke out laughing.

"What may I ask is so funny?"

"Sweetheart, there is only Clara, you and I in the house. My so-called mistress is probably home in bed with her husband. As for Clara, she drank so much tonight it would take a dozen demons to wake her up. So go ahead. Scream your lungs out if it makes you happy."

"Husband?"

"Yes, my dear, her husband. We've been good friends for years. They have a small house on the other side of the compound."

"Is he also Indian?" Sara asked, feeling every bit the fool.

"Yes, they're of the Kansa tribe, if that means anything to you."

"I'm sorry. I thought—"

He leaned down and kissed her nose. "I'm flattered that you were jealous."

Brody had to grin at how quickly her ire rose. "Oh, mouse, you're such a contradiction. Why are you so afraid to let me see inside you?" He rolled on his back, taking her with him. She sat straddling his waist. The look on her face clearly showed that she had no idea what to do next.

Brody didn't need to have his question about Malcolm answered. He'd already figured out the answers. Her lover probably hadn't known how to control himself so he'd had her lie still.

"Give me your hands," he said gently.

Sara did as she was told. He placed them on his chest. "See, I don't break and I don't crumble. I derive as much pleasure when you touch me as I do when I touch you."

He reached up and cupped her breasts in his hands. "You have wonderful breasts. I want to suckle one, and have you press my head against you, not wanting me to stop."

Sara sucked in her breath. She'd never had a man speak to her so openly of such matters.

"Now it's your turn."

How could she talk when he'd just placed her nipple between his finger and thumb and was now rubbing his thumb over the sensitive area? "What do you mean?" she finally managed to asked.

"Tell me what you feel."

"I don't know."

"Does the hair on my chest bother you? Does my skin feel rough? Do you want to rub your hands over my shoulders?" He raised up, keeping her astride him and took a rosy bud into his mouth. He trailed his tongue to the hollow her of neck. "Come on, Sara, tell me what you feel."

Sara had to stop and think. "Everywhere you touch sets my skin on fire."

Sara felt brazen, but with Brody making her talk about her pleasures and needs, she seemed to come alive. Any inhibitions were quickly removed. She felt no shame in confessing her need for him and as he stoked the inferno, she had no trouble telling him that his mouth and hands were driving her to insanity.

"Please, Brody," she begged, "enter me before you can no longer perform."

"That's something you have no need to worry about," he answered, his voice husky with desire.

"Brody, please. I'll die if you don't—" Sara didn't know how to say it. "I've only known satisfaction a couple of times and—"

Brody rolled her onto her back and she gladly spread her legs for him. He entered her slowly, filling her completely. Like a woman possessed, she reached behind him and pressed against his hips forcing him to give her what she wanted so desperately.

The heavens opened, taking her to heights of pleasure she never knew existed. Brody's kisses were sweet nectar and she threw her arms around his neck, passionately returning them, her nails digging into his back. He made her feel like a woman, a very desired woman, and she gloried in the pleasure of it.

Suddenly she fell back, her breath coming in gasps. She was falling off a mountain—

"Oh, Brody," she finally said, "I've never known anything—"

"But we're not through."

She couldn't believe he still had her on a crest that kept getting higher and higher. She couldn't talk, she couldn't breathe. "Please," she uttered, "don't stop. I—"

Sara heard what sounded like a scream in the distance as wave after wave of indescribable pleasure consumed her. Had that been her?

After spending most of the night making love, Sara fell into a peaceful sleep just before dawn. Brody smiled with satisfaction. The wait for Sara to come around had been well worth it. He had released a tiger, and on this night the tiger and the lion had finally mated.

Chapter Fifteen

Sara wasn't quite sure whether it had been the sun shining through the open window or the time of morning that awakened her. Feeling like a pampered feline, she stretched, and yes, there was indeed a smile on her face.

She ran her hand across her breast. Last night had been the most glorious night of her life. Brody had known exactly how to make her body come alive. Time and again he'd taken her from one climax to another, until she was too exhausted to stay awake.

It wasn't only his looks that made women cling to him. Just the thought of him making love to others was like choking on a rusty sword that had been jammed down her throat.

Had she known what it would be like having Brody make love to her, she would never have put him off for so long. She thought a minute. That wasn't true. If she'd known what pleasures were in store, she'd still be running. He'd made her into a wanton woman who couldn't wait until he made love to her again.

She glanced around her room. Brody had to have carried her here. She giggled. She'd been too exhausted to wake up. But when had he brought her here? Did anyone know what happened last night?

"My dear," Clara exclaimed upon seeing Sara entering the great room, "you look absolutely radiant this morning. You must have taken my suggestion about the chamomile tea before bed, or maybe Brody was right about you needing to sleep late. Especially after all the time you'd spent working with Buckets, plus the dancing you did at yesterday's party. I certainly needed rest. I've only been up less than an hour."

Sara expelled a sigh of relief. Clara knew nothing about what had happened after the party.

"Did Brody sleep late also?" Sara hoped she hadn't sounded eager to see him. She poured herself a cup of coffee and joined Clara at the table.

"Kapata said he was up at four-thirty this morning and had breakfast with the cowhands. He did stick his head in the door only minutes ago to see if you were still sleeping."

That he'd taken the trouble to inquire about her made Sara's day all the brighter.

"He said to let him know when you wanted to try saddling Buckets." Sara's elation plummeted. Did he actually want to know about her or was he anxious to get rid of her, now that he'd taken her to his bed? They'd spent long hours talking and making love last night, but nothing had been discussed about the future. She'd simply assumed... How very naive of her to have assumed anything. Brody might make love to her, but she'd always known he would never return any feelings she had for him.

As Brody held the saddle in front of Buckets so the mare would familiarize herself with it, Brody was reminded of the circumstance that had led him to purchase the mare. True, he'd never seen a paint like her. She was sleek, with fine lines and good space between her eyes. But the mare didn't like women. The owner had told him so. That's why he'd been willing to pay such a high price.

Brody chuckled at how right he'd been about Sara's reaction once she'd laid eyes on the mare. Just as he'd planned, once she'd set her mind to owning the horse she had been committed to returning to the ranch, right where he'd wanted her.

All morning he'd fought the urge to join her in her bed. He'd been very tempted to leave her in his bed this morning and let Clara discover their night of passion. It would have put a quick stop to sneaking around. After all, they weren't children stealing the old man's cigar and hiding in the shed to smoke it. Unfortunately it would have also driven Sara from his bed again, and he'd gone to too much trouble to get her there.

The mare trotted off, grabbed a mouthful of oats and returned. Again she smelled the saddle.

Brody chuckled, thoughts of making love to Sara still on his mind. He'd actually expected her to be coy during their first night together instead of being un-inhibited. But apparently, as with everything else she did in her life, once committed to something, she didn't look back. The beauty had freely and wantonly partaken in their pleasure.

"You seem to be in deep thought."

Brody looked up and saw Sara standing by the gate. Her hair had been pulled back with a scarf and she looked very appealing in her buckskin vest and wide-legged pants that looked more like a skirt. Jacob, the tanner had told him of Sara's request and had wanted to know if it would be all right.

"Good morning." Hell's fire! Just looking at her had him thinking about last night.

"Shall I open the gate and come in? Is it safe?"

"There's probably no need to worry about Buckets, but you damn sure should worry about me."

Sara's mood brightened as his eyes covered every inch of her. Being admired by a very masculine man brought life into her soul. She grinned and entered the corral. "Pray tell, sir, what will you do to me?"

"Ravish you."

"Now?"

He chuckled. "Right here and now if I thought I could get away with it."

Tiny beads of perspiration broke out between Sara's breasts. "That would be impossible. I mean... someone could walk up and see us." She licked her lips, wanting him to make love to her again.

Buckets's neighing broke the spell.

To Sara's delight, the mare had actually come to her and nuzzled her shoulder. Sara slowly extended her hand and Buckets allowed her muzzle to be rubbed.

"We've won," she crooned, making sure she didn't raise her voice.

"Let's see if she'll let you on her back. If she does, we can go for a ride."

After successfully placing the saddle blanket on Buckets's back, Brody lifted up the saddle, letting the mare smell it first. "Are you sure you want to use this little thing?" Brody asked Sara.

"If I'm to ride, I might as well do it properly."

"If you say so." Brody swung the saddle up and positioned it, then reach under the mare's belly to tighten the cinch. "So far so good." He looked at Sara. "Ready to give it a try?"

Sara took a deep breath. "Yes."

"Don't be disappointed if we have to do this more than once."

"I won't."

Brody lifted her into the saddle. Buckets became stiff-legged.

"You're such a pretty girl," Sara crooned. She reached out and caressed the thick, glossy neck.

When nothing happened, Sara carefully raised her leg and placed it around the pommel. Still Buckets didn't move. Sara continued the petting and also began humming an old Irish tune her grandfather had taught her many years ago. Slowly Buckets relaxed.

"Apparently she's willing to give you a try. Why don't you rein her around the corral several times?"

After a successful tryout, Sara looked proudly at Brody. "I think we can go now."

"Like I said once before, you do have a way with horses."

"And men?" Sara felt quite saucy.

The couple rode for nearly thirty minutes at a brisk pace, allowing Buckets to stretch her legs. Sara found the mare to be high-spirited, but easily handled.

When they came to a large pond, Brody brought them to a halt and dismounted. He reached up to help Sara down and she gladly went into his arms. In the few seconds it took to tether the horses, Sara had already removed her vest and untied the waist of her britches where they lay in a puddle at her feet.

Brody smiled at seeing the lack of undergarments. "You must have anticipated my need. Or was it your need you were thinking about?" He took her in his arms and to his delight, she unbuttoned his shirt and kissed his naked chest.

"Both."

Her words tickled his skin. "Dear, sweet Sara," he moaned as she unbuttoned his trousers, "you are indeed a pleasure worth waiting for."

Sara's tongue followed her hands downward.

Satiated and feeling safe in the harbor of Brody's arms, Sara lay contentedly and listened to his deep breathing. This time he had fallen asleep, but she didn't mind. Their need for one another had been so strong that it was equivalent to a forest fire, the wind blowing the fire out of control. They'd needed no foreplay. Only the joining of their bodies could extinguish their need.

Now what am I going to do? Sara wondered. Her love for him had become so strong it scared her. God have mercy on her. If he were to ask her to jump in a river and drown, she'd probably be stupid enough to do it. He had taken the fight out of her, he'd even reached down and taken her very soul. But she'd known all along that he wouldn't settle for anything less. She was indeed bedeviled.

She thought back to when he'd first entered her office so long ago. The minute she'd laid eyes on him she'd become entangled in his web. She'd thought she could play with fire and not be burned. Was there ever a more naive woman than she'd been? She'd certainly been warned to stay away from him. Now she had set herself up for heartache. How long would it be before he started looking at other women?

His hand moved up and cupped her breast. She leaned against him, drawing pleasure from his touch. How long could she keep him interested?

"Have I told you you have lips as sweet as cherries?"

Brody's compliments were as warming as a coat in the dead of winter. "You have now."

Though Sara felt guilty, she told Clara that to be sure Buckets really had come around to trusting her, she decided to spend an extra two days at the ranch. Clara was delighted. So for the next four days, she and Brody went for long rides and made love in the deep buffalo grass. At night she stole into Brody's room, then crept back to her own just as dawn broke.

Sara floated among the clouds, her feet never touching the ground.

Chapter Sixteen

Brody downed his shot of Irish whiskey, which the waiter immediately replaced with another. The amenities at the Bucket of Ale were as good or better than any men's club he'd been in.

"And just how much of our business is the railroad going to take away?" Lester asked, his forehead creased in a deep frown.

"That's what we'll find out in Washington," Casey Riggs replied.

Brody lit his cigar and settled back in his chair. "It's not going to affect us for a long time to come. Nevertheless, I still think you'd all be wise to invest in this railroad venture."

"Are you going to?"

"I'm investing a considerable amount. I'm convinced it's going to change life as we know it today. But we'll give you all the details when we return and you can make up your own minds."

* * *

Sara was at a loss for words when Patricia Riggs arrived at Miles Freight Company.

"I hope this isn't at an inopportune time to come calling," Patricia drawled with a faint smile. She glanced around the small office. "I needed to talk to you and I never seem to be able to catch you at home."

Without waiting for an invitation, she sat in one of the wooden chairs facing Sara's desk.

"Your seamstress is such a wonder," Sara commented. She moved a stack of invoices to the side, giving her time to collect herself. "Your town suit is very becoming and the color is perfect." Why would Patricia make such an unexpected appearance?

Patricia patted the back of her head, her smug smile spread over small, even white teeth. A gesture she often did when a compliment had been given. Sara knew quite well that Patricia spent over an hour each morning just looking in the mirror and supervising her personal maid's attempt at the perfect coiffeur.

"Yes. As you know, I wear pink quite often for that very reason." She removed a lacy white handkerchief from her reticule and dabbed her nose. "I haven't seen you in several months. I think the last time was at Nallie Wooten's ball."

"Yes. I believe you're right."

"I felt so sorry for you that night."

"Why?"

Patricia leaned forward, as if confiding a secret. "Why? Really, Sara, having to put up with Brody must have been terribly difficult. Especially the way he followed you around and didn't allow old acquaintances an opportunity to dance with you. But of course he can be terribly dominating. Everyone knew he'd found some way to force you to accompany him."

"He didn't force me." Would she ever be forgiven for all her lies? "He sent me an invitation and I accepted."

Patricia leaned back in her chair. "Well, I'll be. Now he has you under his spell also."

"Also?"

"It happens to every woman he chooses to take under his wing...so to speak," Patricia said sadly. "I thought you, of all people, would be immune."

"Why? You aren't immune."

"No, that's why I know what he's like." Patricia smoothed her silk skirt, trying to get control of her discomfort. "You're undoubtedly wondering why I'm here. Quite honestly, guilt brought me here."

"What guilt?"

"In all fairness, I could no longer stand back and watch Brody take advantage of you." She lowered her eyes, her thick lashes resting against alabaster cheeks. "This isn't easy for me to say." She twisted her handkerchief into a corkscrew. "Sara, you have every right to know that Brody and I have been deeply in love for several years."

Sara stopped breathing.

"More than once Brody has asked me to leave Casey. I won't, so he taunts me by being with other women. I'm ashamed to say I tend to do the same with other men just to get back at him." She looked at Sara, her face drawn. "I've been afraid all along that he'd come after you once we became close friends. Trust me when I tell you he'd go to any extreme to make me jealous and leave Casey."

"I don't believe a word you've said," Sara protested. She stood, hoping Patricia would take the hint and leave.

"Do you remember when you told me Brody was snubbing you?"

Sara nodded. "Patricia, I'm very busy and—"

"Sara, I don't want to hurt you, but things could end up far worse if I choose to remain silent. Didn't you wonder why, for no particular reason, Brody suddenly turned his sights on you? There's no doubt in my mind that he deliberately set out to seduce you. And not obviously. Oh, no. That wouldn't be his style. The fun for him is not letting you know that every move had been carefully planned."

Sara thought about Buckets. Had it been a deliberate ploy on Brody's part? "If you love Brody, why do you stay with Casey?" Sara asked, suddenly feeling weak.

Patricia let out a deep, heartrending sigh. "I'm afraid they'd end up killing each other," she whispered. "And I couldn't stand the thought of Casey taking my children from me." Patricia dabbed at the moisture that had formed in her blue eyes.

"What finally brought me to see you were the several social functions you and Brody have attended, plus the numerous occasions you've been seen riding together. I know that what goes on between the two of you shouldn't be any of my business, but you've become so dear to me I hate the thought of you ending up with a broken heart."

Sara's mouth had turned to sawdust.

"I'm sorry for the times I've snapped at you, Sara," Patricia said softly, "but jealousy often makes me a witch. And while I'm letting the truth be known, everyone suspects our relationship—"

"Relationship?"

Patricia nodded as she cast her eyes on the floor in shame. "But no one could ever prove it," she concluded.

Brody had used the same words when he'd suggested a cabin in the woods where they could meet.

Her eyes rimmed with tears, Patricia looked up at Sara. "I'm so sorry I've waited so long to confide in you, but I honestly thought you were immune to Brody's charms. I should have known better."

Sara cleared her throat. "I don't want to discuss it."

"But you didn't deny it. I'm incapable of casting stones, Sara, because I did have an affair with him, and I still love him so much that I hurt just looking at him." Patricia slowly stood. "I'm afraid I've said far too much, so I'll leave. I know you won't want to visit me anymore, and that saddens me even more. Loving Brody has cost me much, including your friendship.

"Sara, please believe me, I'm not trying to be hurtful, but I must tell you everyone is gossiping about the beautiful horse Brody gave you, and making innuendoes as to what you did to deserve such a handsome gift."

Sara forced herself to stand straight. Patricia would never know how deeply her words had hurt. "Why do they think it's a gift from Brody?"

"My mother-in-law couldn't wait to tell the others about it, and you know how gossip flies, especially with those four."

Patricia went to the door and opened it a crack before once again turning to Sara. "He hasn't asked you to marry him, has he? For your own sake, my dear, don't convince yourself that I'm lying and that it's you Brody loves. On the other hand, Brody can be very unpredictable. He once told me he wanted to expand and that he intended to buy out Hamish Goodman. I'm sure you've learned by now that when Brody wants something he lets nothing stand in his way. He knows I'll not leave my children, so why not marry you? He'd not only have Hamish Goodman's company, he'd have yours as well."

She swung the door open and left.

Sara collapsed onto the chair.

* * *

Even after a night of making love, Sara lay wide-awake on the hard bed, softened by a thick feather mattress Brody had provided. Ever since they'd left the ranch, they had met at the small log cabin Brody claimed he and his Indian friend, Felaytay, used when they went hunting. It was ideal because of its seclusion and close proximity to town. As Brody had explained, no one would see anything that might compromise her reputation.

Sara released a heavy sigh. She continued to get herself deeper and deeper into a situation that had no happy ending, but she was so madly in love that the thought of never being with Brody again was more than she could bear.

"Is something wrong?" Brody tightened his arms around her and pulled her against him.

"Why do you think something's wrong?"

"The way you sighed, your restlessness, not to mention your lack of sleep tonight. Has anything happened that I should know about?"

Sara thought of Patricia's visit two days ago. She was tempted to confront Brody with what Patricia had said. But if Patricia had told the truth, Brody would deny it with lies. "No, I was just wondering about some things." It wasn't easy to hide anything from Brody. He seemed to have a sixth sense when it came to her thoughts.

"Like what?"

"I was wondering if our being together had anything to do with some scheme you'd concocted."

Brody rolled onto his back, deliberating on how to answer the question. He certainly wasn't going to tell he'd deliberately stripped her buggy at the ranch. "Every man plans ways of getting to know a woman."

A knot balled up in Sara's chest. Hadn't Patricia said basically the same thing? "You snubbed me. What made you change your mind?"

Brody had long since decided not to tell Sara just how far he'd gone to entice her to his bed. "Your stubborn determination intrigued me."

"Even after learning about Malcolm?"

Brody moved her around until her head rested on his broad chest. "Sara, you had an affair with a rake of a man, but that doesn't make you a loose woman." He stroked her thick hair, a soft chuckle coming from his chest. "How could I let you turn away from me when you were such a beautiful temptress? I wanted you right here beside me."

"What about Buckets? Was she part of your scheme to get me into your bed?"

"Why would you think there was any kind of a scheme? Like I told you, I saw her and thought of you. Nothing more. Why are you suddenly making so much of all this?"

"Just curious. Did you know that everyone is aware

that Buckets is a gift from you and the gossips are conjuring up all sorts of rumors about us?''

"So I've heard, but they've no proof of anything."

The same words Patricia had used about her affair with him. Sara climbed off the bed. "I have been told our little affair is your way of making a particular woman jealous."

"And pray tell, what woman am I trying to make jealous?"

"A name wasn't mentioned." Obviously he had no intention of telling her about Patricia. She had to be careful not to let him find out that their relationship meant far more to her than just a casual fling.

"You know," Sara said with forced lightheartedness, "even though we've made love, it doesn't changes anything between us."

"What do you mean?"

"I'll still take every opportunity to further my business even if it means stepping on your toes."

Brody sat up and scooted to the edge of the bed, a wide grin spread across his face. "I wouldn't have it any other way. Now come here and I'll lace your corset."

Sara went to him and turned her back. "A man of many talents. I've never had a gentleman dress me."

Brody chuckled at her play on words. "Tell me, Sara," he said as he tightened the strings, "are you a natural tease when it comes to men or is it something you've worked at perfecting?"

"When a young woman is constantly watched over by a caring but strict father, plus a brother of equal purpose, she quickly learns how to get her way when possible. Oh! Don't pull so tight."

"Before you leave, I want you to lie down beside me for a minute. I have something to tell you."

His serious tone stopped Sara from refusing. Maybe he was about to confess after all. But did she really want to hear it?

He scooted over so she'd have enough room. "I'm leaving this morning for Washington and I won't be back for about a month."

Sara turned onto her side, facing him. The lanterns were turned down low but she could still see him clearly. "A month?" Could she bear to be away from him that long? "Why have you waited until now to tell me?"

"I didn't want to ruin our last night together." He kissed her nose. "I'll miss you."

Sara closed her eyes, holding back the tears. She hadn't expected him to say something so endearing. Could she possibly make him forget Patricia and fall in love with her?

"Can I trust you to be good while I'm gone?" he teased.

Sara opened her eyes and smiled. "Can I trust you? You do have a flare for women." His sea-green eyes held her captive. He trailed his finger along her eyebrows, as if putting them to memory. Sara laughed with delight at seeing his features warm with passion. "I probably shouldn't have bothered putting my corset on."

"I was thinking the very same thing." He placed his arm over her hips and drew her closer to him. "It's already nearing dawn, and I want to leave with the sweet taste of you in my mouth."

The sky had paled and a nightingale had started its serenading by the time Sara hurriedly dressed. "Maybe with you gone I can get some work done," Sara joked. "Time has passed so quickly that it's hard to believe winter is practically upon us."

"Have I ever told you how much I enjoy watching you dress?"

"No, but don't stop." Sara laughed and watched him leave the bed. He had never been shy about his nakedness. "Why are you going to Washington?"

"I'm meeting with some gentlemen who are discussing the plausibility of moving the railroad west."

Sara tied a bow with her slip strings. "But that will hurt the freighting business."

"The forts, Santa Fe and other outside areas will be using freighting for many years to come. The railroad can only cover distance, but not necessarily a large area."

Sara finished hooking the front of her violet waist-length jacket. "Are you going alone?" She looked in the mirror while making an attempt at plaiting her hair.

"No. Casey and Patricia Riggs will be accompanying me."

Sara's hands stilled. "Why is Patricia going?"

"You know as well as I do that Patricia isn't going to miss an opportunity to go shopping."

"I'm sure." Sara held on to the base stand and studied Brody's profile in the mirror. She wanted to scream at him, tell him she knew what he was up to and call him every foul name she could think of. As if to rub salt in her wound, there wasn't a single trace of guilt on his face.

He epitomized the perfect lover. Quick with little endearing words while making love, saying he'd miss her and even commenting on how he enjoyed watching her dress. Yes, he knew how to make a woman feel very special, even if his words were filled with lies.

Grabbed by a sudden urge to be alone, Sara quickly finished dressing. She needed the early-morning air to cool her heated cheeks and rid the cobwebs fogging her mind. She needed to escape before she began bawling. No matter what, he wouldn't take away her pride and she wouldn't grovel.

"I'll see you when you return." Sara slung the wool cape over her shoulders.

"Wait." Brody stepped in front of the door. "Something's wrong."

Sara buried her hands in the folds of her cape and forced a smile. "Why should there be?"

"Pretending won't work, sweetheart. I know you too well. You're upset." He cocked a dark brow. "Why? Because I'm going to be gone? Because I didn't ask you to go with me?"

"Don't flatter yourself. You know I couldn't or wouldn't go. Maybe that's why you didn't ask. And while you're gone, I'll not refuse an invitation to attend some social function. I'm quite certain you'll be attending parties."

His lean, sober expression almost made Sara confront him with the truth. "Actually, I'm glad you're leaving." She looked him straight in the eye. "Maybe I can finally catch up on my sleep as well. Even Clara was saying I look haggard." She wasn't as good at lying as he was, but she was getting there.

Brody studied her for a long moment. She hadn't spoken the truth, but he couldn't detain her any longer. It was already becoming light outside. He leaned down and gently kissed her swollen lips. "Until my return."

Sara nodded. "Until your return," she replied, her words mere whispers.

Brody stepped aside. Sara left.

Instead of burying herself in work, Sara spent the following week sequestered in her room. Lucas came by several times, but the housekeeper had informed him that Sara was sick and couldn't see anyone.

When not crying, Sara bemoaned her fate. She

thrashed pillows, ripped sheets, and threw things, none of which helped to alleviate her misery.

For long moments, Sara hated Brody. He was a calculating womanizer who cared nothing about the feelings of the women he left behind. He made them fall in love with him and gave nothing in return. He didn't know the meaning of love...except for Patricia.

Then there were the periods of hating herself for being so weak; for still wanting to feel his touch, his kisses.

By the time Sara left her room, she'd come to accept the glaring reality of her situation. Whether it was now or later, the end of their affair was inevitable. In the back of her mind she'd known all along that it couldn't last. Eventually the time would come when having Brody make love to her wouldn't be enough. Perhaps that was why she'd held out for so long before giving in to her passion.

Nothing would change Brody. She may love him but she didn't like him. But even knowing what he was like, she still wanted him. She'd been cursed with a love that would last the rest of her life. But she couldn't exist on her love alone.

She needed to be needed.

She needed for him to want to take care of her.

She wanted him to think of her with every breath he took.

She desperately wanted him to love her.

Sara had finally concluded that being with Brody

had been the most wonderful experience of her life. She had no expectations of finding another man who could equal his prowess in bed. And in fairness to him, he'd never mentioned any sort of a future between them. She'd gone into this with her eyes open. She'd known his reputation. She'd persisted in testing the water until she'd finally drowned.

Chapter Seventeen

At work, Sara sat looking down at the figures in the ledger with unseeing eyes. How long would it take to stop thinking about Brody?

The numbers came back into view and for another five minutes she concentrated on tallying the shipping bills. A wicked laugh suddenly escaped her lips. What would Brody's reaction be when he discovered an older, wiser woman had replaced the naive creature he thought he could lead around by the nose? Happy because he and Patricia could be together or determined to continue his affair with her? It really didn't matter. She'd finally found the strength to end their relationship. For once, he'd be the rejected one. He'd have to find someone else to make Patricia jealous.

"Sara, are you busy?

Sara looked up and saw Lucas standing in the doorway. "No. Come on in."

"I've got someone with me. Name's Blacky and says he has something to tell you."

A short, pox-faced man followed Lucas into the room. Blacky kept wringing his hat in his hands. Sara waited for the stranger to say something.

The man looked at Lucas.

"Go ahead," Lucas commanded.

"Well, ma'am, as Lucas told you, my name's Blacky—"

"Hello, Blacky."

"Get on with it," Lucas said impatiently.

He shuffled his feet. "Since Mr. Hawkins is out of town, I thought I could return a favor Lucas did for me some months ago."

Sara placed her elbows on the desk, her interest piqued. "Go on."

"I'm the only survivor of Mr. Hawkins's outfit that had been returning on the Oregon Trail. Injuns got us two days ago."

Sara slowly rose. "What are you trying to say?"

Lucas shoved the man aside. "He's saying there's twenty wagons of goods just sitting, waiting for someone to claim them."

Excitement shot through her veins like quicksilver. "What condition are they in? Are they movable or would the goods have to be transferred to other wagons?"

"They're just sittin'. Injuns wanted the mules, not the goods." Blacky shifted his weight to his other foot.

"During the attack, the wagons were pulled behind a hill and no one would see them lest they knew they was there. Anyone could take a team out there, hook 'em up and go."

"How far away?"

"About half the distance from here to Fort Kearny. Not far."

"And you'll lead Lucas and the mule skinners there?"

"Yes'm." Blacky jammed his hat back on his head but seeing the look Lucas gave him, he snatched it back off.

Sara paced the floor, her mind racing. "Can we get mule skinners, Lucas?"

He nodded.

"What about stock?"

"I have the stock now that the last wagons are in."

Sara came to an abrupt halt, her face lit up as bright as any Christmas tree. "Lucas, we're about to make a big bundle of money with no output."

"You're not going to do it as a helping hand?" Lucas asked, a deep frown creasing his wide forehead.

Sara sobered. "I feel as bad about the loss of the men as I would if they were mine. But I can't change that."

Lucas nodded.

"Nor can I turn my nose on an opportunity to show Mr. Hawkins that contrary to what he thinks, I'm quite capable of taking care of myself."

"I don't know, Sara—"

"I can't wait to see the look on Brody's face. And it's legal. Get busy, Lucas. I want those wagons emptied and sold by the time Mr. Hawkins returns."

Sara clapped her hands, still finding her unexpected good fortune hard to believe. Even if the goods had spoiled, she'd still make a huge profit. Mr. Hawkins had a big surprise awaiting his return. Apparently she wasn't as forgiving as she'd thought.

Chapter Eighteen

Sara kept Buckets at an easy lope as they followed a wide path parallel to the river. Buckets needed the exercise and Sara hoped the sun and fresh air would improve her disposition. As Brody's return loomed closer, her nervousness had increased. Patience had become a forgotten word and on more than one occasion she'd snapped at a worker without reason. Even Lucas had felt the sting of her discord.

The money she'd put away from the sale of Brody's goods continued to haunt her. Though she still considered it a fair means of getting even for Brody using her, she knew he would have an entirely different outlook on the matter. She'd discussed the situation with Hamish, who still hadn't left Leavenworth, but he'd only made her more squeamish.

"Now there's one man you ain't wantin' on your bad side, girl. I heard tell that he'd killed more than one man who'd crossed him. That and his size is one reason why crooked men don't mess with him." Hamish had shook his head, his face mirroring his concern. "But for as long as I've known him, he's always run an honest business and he keeps his prices fair."

"But what I did was perfectly legal."

"Brody is his own law, mouse," he'd said kindly. "You got no choice now but to wait and see how he reacts to you claiming his goods."

Sara slowed Buckets to a walk. She could not continue to allow Brody to intimidate her. She'd been walking on needles and he hadn't even returned from Washington yet. At this rate she'd make herself sick. If only she could move time forward and put all this behind her once and for all. Maybe then her normally good disposition would return.

As the week passed, Sara made a point of being nice to her employees, trying to make up for how she'd treated them. She didn't want to act surly. She even began smiling when she reached the office...until one of her clerks informed her that around seven that morning, he'd seen Mr. Hawkins enter his building.

All morning, Sara sat at her desk waiting. Work of any kind was impossible. By noon, she started pacing the floor. At three o'clock, she was exhausted. But Brody had answered the questions that had been running through her mind. It was obvious he'd convinced Patricia to see things his way or he would have already made it across the street. And he wasn't going to confront her about the wagons. All of which should have relieved her. It didn't. She wanted to hear him say it. Besides, she wanted the opportunity to refuse him should he want her to return to his bed.

Sara had given up on Brody coming to see her and was preparing to go home when the unpredictable man finally made an appearance.

"You look like you're angry at me." Brody smiled. "I've been in meetings all day with Riggs, Kestrel, Wooten, Gilbert and some other freighters. Casey and I have been telling the others what took place in Washington."

Sara walked over to the small window and looked out. It was that time of year when darkness kept creeping up earlier and earlier. "How is Patricia?"

"Fine."

She wanted to slap him. She couldn't bring herself to ask any more questions about the woman. "Why didn't you include me in the meeting?" His good mood made her suspect he hadn't found out about the wagons yet.

"I wanted to tell you about it when we were alone. Will you meet me at the cabin tonight?"

So he hadn't talked Patricia into leaving Casey. Sara turned and studied the tall, handsome man, his black hair windblown as it had been the day they'd first met. It would be so easy to rush to the cabin and once again feel his arms around her. He had taken away her willpower to resist him, but by using her, he'd given it back.

"No, I won't be going to the cabin, now or ever."

"Oh?"

Sara watched his lean face turn to stone.

"May I ask why?"

Sara crossed her arms over her bodice. This wasn't as easy as she'd anticipated. "I want to end our relationship, Brody."

"Is there another man?"

"No." Her eyes downcast, Sara uncrossed her arms and smoothed the front of her linen dress. "I hope you're gentleman enough to accept my decision without tossing questions at me."

"And how long will it be before you change your mind again?"

Sara stood tall, her brown eyes flashing with indignation. "That's something you're not going to have to worry about. Tell me, what do you say to women when you want to get rid of them?"

A lopsided grin slowly spread across his mouth. "I guess that's something you'll never know." He gave her a nod and left.

Sara remained looking out the window, watching Brody cross the street. The only thing left of her heart were shards. Remnants of something wonderful. The long rides together, the joining of their bodies, the whispered words, even their talks when she would tell him things about her past were gone. In times to come, she'd probably forget the bad and remember only the good.

She turned and glanced around the room. A vast improvement from when she'd first looked at it. Now it was clean and everything in its proper place. Like her life. She took a deep breath and slowly let it out. Though pained by their parting, she felt good about herself. For the first time since meeting Brody, she'd stood on her two feet and did what she knew to be right. Had she waited until he'd ended their affair, there wouldn't have even been shards left.

Early the following morning, Sara's attention was drawn from the manifest she'd been reading by the deep voice coming from the other room.

"Is she in her office?"

Brody had returned, and from the sound of his voice, he was madder than a hornet. He'd found out about the wagons. Sara sat straight in her chair and waited. When Brody stormed in, the cold, thunderous look on his face told her her hopes had been dashed. He hadn't taken the news well. She raised her chin, ready to go to battle.

"I just found out why, before I left, you acted so strange and felt the need to remind me that we're in competition."

His cold, emotionless face frightened her. Even so, she glared unflinchingly at him. "The cargo was up for grabs. I just got there first."

He placed his knuckles on the desk and leaned forward, staring down at her. "And would you care to tell me how you knew the cargo was available?" The muscles in his jaws twitched and his voice was deadly quiet.

"I—I don't have to explain a thing to you."

Brody's big fist hit the top of the desk. Sara jumped and journals and paper fell to the floor.

"The hell you don't, lady. Was coming to my bed also part of a charade? Then when you had what you wanted, you ended it." He leaned even closer to her face. "I honestly didn't give you the credit you deserve. Did you actually think that because I'd made love to you, I'd willingly let you get away with this? I want some answers and I want them right now."

"You're overreacting."

"Be damn glad that's all I'm doing!"

Sara had expected him to be angry, in fact she'd counted on it. But she hadn't expected such deadly fierceness. "I did nothing more than you would have done were the circumstances reversed."

"You told me you'd do most any thing to get business, but lady, you picked the wrong man to mess with this time. You not only had my wagons waylaid," he snarled, "you had thirty good men murdered."

Sara jumped to her feet. "That's not true," she gasped. "How could you even think I'd do such a thing?"

"Don't even bother using that innocent look. Who claimed the salvage?"

"W-well, I did."

"And just how did you manage to claim it only a day after it happened?"

"I didn't. That would be impossible."

"Unless it was your men who committed the slaughter."

"How dare you accuse me of such a thing?"

"What happened to the bodies?"

"Lucas said there were only twenty-five, and he had them buried. He didn't know where the others were."

"Whose idea was it to hijack the wagons, Sara? Yours or your wagon master's? My leaving for Washington must have blended perfectly with your scheme."

"I said I had nothing to do with it! The killings were committed before we took the wagons. Now either you believe me or you don't." The injustice of his accusations sent her temper soaring. "I refuse to stand here defending myself when you don't even want to listen." She would not let him see how deeply his accusations hurt.

"Sara, do you want me to throw him out?"

Sara and Brody turned at the same time, seeing Lucas in the doorway.

"Thank you, Lucas," Sara said, relieved by his timely arrival, "but I don't think it will be necessary. I'm sure Mr. Hawkins has enough sense to leave quietly."

"Have you been listening, Lucas?" Brody asked.

"I heard enough."

"Then maybe you'd like to tell me how Sara planned all this while I was gone? It beats finding your neck in a noose. Or perhaps you'd like to confess to your—"

Lucas put his head down and charged.

Sara screamed.

Anticipating Lucas's move, Brody deftly maneuvered off to the side. Lucas's bull weight carried him into the ceiling-high bookcase.

Sara clasped her hands over her mouth. Fortunately Lucas didn't appear hurt, just momentarily stunned. She quickly looked to the doorway for help at ending this. Even she could see her employees were pathetically scrawny and would undoubtedly end up dead if they tried to interfere with the two big men.

The ledgers and other objects had fallen on top of Lucas, but he was quick to rise to his feet. This time he hunkered down, kept his eyes on Brody, and moved slowly forward. The rage and contempt on each man's face sent icicles up Sara's spine.

Brody yanked off his waistcoat and tossed it to the side. "Are you sure you want to do this, Lucas?" he asked with a half-cocked grin.

"You've been askin' for it ever since Sara came here. It's time you got put in your place."

"I haven't had a good fight in some time. I hope you don't disappoint me."

Sara reached to grab her gun from the drawer, but as Brody passed by, he shoved the heavy desk back, pinning her to the wall. Sara couldn't understand why Brody didn't move away as Lucas approached. He wasn't going to have any teeth by the time her wagon master finished with him. But suddenly Brody brought his big fist down and up, delivering a hard, brutal uppercut to Lucas's chin, sending Lucas staggering backward, but he didn't fall.

Sara finally managed to squeeze from behind the desk as Brody delivered another hard blow, then another to the jaw.

Sara was about to run to the doorway, when Lucas, shaking his head, came forward and grabbed Brody around the waist in a bear hug. Not satisfied, he raised Brody's feet off the floor then slammed the big man down on Sara's desk, snapping it in half. Brody fell to the floor with Lucas on top of him.

Sara scooted off in the other direction. She didn't want to watch, yet she couldn't take her eyes off the savage fight. Lucas's nose had been broken, and blood seemed to be everywhere. Powerful blows continued to be exchanged, each loud smack of a big fist tearing her heart out. She didn't want kind, sweet Lucas to be beat up, and even after Brody's accusations, she couldn't stand seeing Brody hurt.

"Stop," Sara yelled, but neither heard her. If only there was another gun available. She tried yelling again and received the same reaction. Then suddenly, the fight was over. Lucas lay on his back, out cold, Brody standing over him. Though his shirt had been torn and blood streaked the front, it looked as if Brody only had a swollen eye and several cuts to the face.

Brody moved away and turned his venom on Sara. "You're not going to get away with this," he growled as he picked up his coat. "You murdered my men and I'm closing you down, sweetheart."

"You have gone too far!" Sara's hands balled into fists, as she rushed forward. "From the very day we met, you have accused me of incompetence. You know nothing about what I can or can't do or the degree of my knowledge. Never once have you taken the time to ask, to offer advice or to provide help. You said your company had more work than it could handle. Did it ever occur to you to send anything my way?"

"Is that what the bed privileges were for?"

Sara slapped his face as hard as she could. "You're like every other smug, self-centered man," she seethed. "The thought of a woman being your equal isn't even worth consideration. Oh, no. Women are for waiting on you, to satisfy your lust or provide sustenance." Sara was practically screaming, but she was past the point of caring.

"From what I recall, your lust was equally satisfied."

"I told you I had nothing to do with your men being waylaid, and you can't prove I did."

"My bullwhacker recognized some of your men."

"Instead of rushing over here with accusations, why

don't you look for the survivor who informed Lucas of the Indian attack? His name was Blacky. A short, pox-faced man. Obviously he had something to do with it and would know who and why. I'd say that from all indications, you aren't the only one who wants to see me close my doors. And who better to do it than the mighty Brody Hawkins? You set me up, didn't you?''

Brody spun around on the heels of his boots and headed for the doorway.

Sara rushed after him. ''Just a minute!''

Brody stopped in his tracks and slowly turned. ''Why? Enough has been said already.''

''Because I'm going to tell you how you can get rid of me once and for all.''

She definitely had Brody's attention. ''I have had my fill of constantly being badgered and belittled. I am very good at what I do, and if you would open your eyes you'd see that.''

''And just what does any of that have to do with getting rid of you?''

His sneer pierced Sara's heart. ''I wish I had a noose. I'd hang you from the nearest tree.''

''You and who else, lady?''

''You think you're so high and mighty and I'm so incompetent, so why don't we find out who's right?''

''What are you talking about?''

''Why don't we have a race to see who runs the fastest and best freight outfit?''

Brody's mouth spread into a villainous smile. "And if you lose?"

"I'll leave."

"Oh, no. If you lose, I take everything *and* you leave."

The clerks stopped trying to act as if they weren't listening.

Sara placed her hands on her hips and held his eyes with hers. She wasn't about to look away and play the guilty dog. "And if I win?"

"That's not going to be an issue."

"And if I win?" Sara demanded.

"I'll turn some business your way."

"What?" she shrieked. "You want me to put up my company for *some business?* Oh, no. You give me seventy-five thousand dollars, turn business my way, and never, never, never try to make me close my doors again!"

"Done!"

Sara was surprised by his quick agreement. Seeing his smug assuredness egged her on. "I want a legal paper spelling out the agreement and conditions."

"Fine."

"Equal wagons and equal weight from here to Santa Fe."

"I'll have my lawyer draw up the papers. He'll be here tomorrow for your signature." He started to turn away then stopped. "I assure you I'm going to find out who was behind the slaughter of my men. No matter who wins, if you're the culprit, you'll pay dearly. I might add that Dusty, the wagon master, had been with me for years. He was a good man and a friend. But I also take each of my men's deaths personally and no one is going to get away unpunished." He turned and left.

"Ma'am?" the young clerk called softly. She remained perfectly still, staring at the unclosed door. "Ma'am," he said again, "I have papers to deliver to the boot factory."

"Then get to it," she snapped. "And make certain you don't tarry."

"Yes, ma'am." John somehow managed to walk out the door instead of running. In all his days, he'd never seen as good a fight nor had he heard anything as exciting as the big wagons racing across country. He couldn't wait to tell everyone.

Sara hurried back to Lucas, who was still out cold.

Brody's long strides quickly took him across the street. As furious as he had been over the death of his men, he'd been equally furious at being duped by a shrimp of a woman. He'd come dangerously close to being judge, jury and executioner for the murder of his men. He'd wanted to take his anger out on someone and Lucas had been at the wrong place at the wrong time.

He opened the door to his building. Actually, the fight had served another purpose besides making sure Lucas didn't threaten him again. It had cleared his brain. When crossing the street, he'd remembered something Sara had said.

Once in his office, Brody went to the window, rubbing his bruised knuckles. Sara had told him to find the man called Blacky, who had informed her of the Indian raid. Odeon Beckman had reported to him that he'd recognized a couple of Sara's men in the attack. All white men, no Indians. Also, if only twenty-five men had truly been buried, what happened to the others?

Who had told the truth? Sara hadn't tried to convince him of an Indian attack. She'd just mentioned it briefly. She had been solemn and angry, and she never could lie worth a damn. Why would she have been so open about something so underhanded? On the other hand, if renegade white men had committed the crime, what had been their purpose? Why didn't they take the freight and sell it? But if they had been Sara's men, then they did take it to sell.

So help him God, if it turned out to be Sara who had been behind the slayings, she'd never see a clear breath again. Brody went back to the door and yanked it open. "Fred!"

The clerk came hurrying forward. "Yes, sir?"

"Where did Odeon Beckman go?"

"I don't know. He took off the minute you left."

"I don't care what it takes, find him. He couldn't have gone far. If he's slipped out of sight, pay stevedores or bullwhackers to help find him."

"Yes, sir." Fred removed his apron.

"I don't want to see your face until you know where he is."

The bespectacled man hurried off.

"Carl!"

The junior clerk hurried forward.

"Inform my lawyer I want to see him here first thing in the morning."

"Yes, sir."

Guilty or not, he'd soon be rid of Sara Miles. No one had ever stirred up as much trouble as she had. Besides, it was past time to enlarge the company, and he'd do exactly that once he owned Miles Freighting.

Brody left again and went directly to where his horse was kept. First he'd find out if anyone at the Miles freight yard had seen or heard Blacky talking to Lucas. He still hadn't ruled out the big man having been in on the attack. After all, word had gone around about Sara giving him a percentage, so it would have meant a considerable amount of money in his pocket.

The Baronesses looked sadly at Sara, sitting quietly, munching a tart.

"Everyone is talking about your openly admitted affair…and the race," Bertha commented before taking a sip of tea.

"My clerks are just spreading unfounded gossip. I fired them all." Sara's hand was shaking too badly to chance picking up her teacup. She'd seen the looks that had passed between the four women. Not for a minute did they believe her.

"Bets are being taken for the race on practically every street corner," Harriet confided, trying to make things more comfortable for Sara.

"There hasn't been this much excitement since you arrived in town," Nallie added.

"Sara, after all the hours you've spent to build your company, why would you want to take a chance at losing it?" Harriet asked with concern.

"Why don't you tell us what this is about?" Clara said kindly. "You know how much we've come to love you and nothing you could do would make us feel any different. You are a sweet loving child and we do so want to help."

"I'm afraid there's nothing you can do to change anything."

Though Sara adamantly refused to admit her affair with Brody, she did tell them about Brody's accusations, the fight and the wager.

"Do you think you can win?" Clara asked worriedly.

Sara nodded. "With Lucas as the wagon master and our top mule skinners, I'm positive of it. Also, Brody's top wagon master, Dusty Adams, was one of the men killed during the raid."

"Nasty business," Clara stated. "Something about all this doesn't ring true."

Nallie shook her head. "I'd say there's a skunk in the woodpile."

"I've tried to make sense of it, but the only conclusion I can come up with is that this is all a means of shutting me down." Sara sat the uneaten portion of the raspberry tart back onto the small plate. "One of my competitors had to have picked Brody's team. They knew he would be the one man who could and would do it. But for the present, that is neither here nor there. Right now, my mind is centered on the race. There is so much to be done and little time to do it.

"I always look forward to our teas, however I won't be joining you until this is all over. You have been my family and I love each of you for all your support."

When Sara left Hattie's house, she headed straight for the freight yard. The papers had been signed and the rules agreed upon for the race. There would be twenty-four freight wagons each, plus the kitchen wagons. Each outfit had to carry a minimum load of three and a half tons. Freight must be disgorged to frontier communities en route, and legitimate bills of lading in proper order. The wagons had to be empty to be counted winner. Neither owner could accompany their outfits, a clause Sara had insisted on. They had their choice of route as well as oxen or mules. The race would start six o'clock Monday morning, the first day of October.

Chapter Nineteen

At five o'clock in the morning, men were already sitting on rooftops, window sashes were all raised and people with anxious faces stood four to five deep along the streets, all waiting for that historical moment when the great wagons departed. The *Missouri Republican* newspaper had touted this as being the race of the century.

It was hard for Sara to just stand back and watch as Lucas made preparations for leaving. But she had done all she could. The Studebaker wagons were loaded with trade goods from the United States and Europe, ample men had been hired, extra stock purchased, fodder for the finest Missouri mules, and plenty of flour, beans, bacon, coffee and sugar for the teamsters. They'd kill buffalo on the way and collect wild greens to go with their meals.

On an outfit, the wagon master was the law. But not just law. He had to be capable of imposing his authority on men who were equally tough. Lucas knew his duties well. He supervised everything, including the careful loading of each wagon so the goods wouldn't shift, making the wagon topple.

That had been the reason for her papa and brother's deaths. That particular wagon master had ended up being hung.

Poor Lucas, Sara thought. None of this had been his fault, yet everything now rested on his shoulders. She suddenly felt guilty at the way she'd been behaving. A wagon master's job was neverending. Though Lucas had done the same thing time and time again, Sara had acted as if she were tied to his belt. She worried over his handling of the bills of laden and stood by his side as the wagons were thoroughly checked and he chose the animals needed.

He hadn't told her which of the two routes he'd be taking or where he planned to camp each night. At least she'd had enough sense not to press the issue. Her brother had told her that the wagon master constantly moved up and down the wagons in addition to reconnoitering and watching for Indians. She'd never thought to ask him how the stops were decided.

The twelve mule teams were now being hitched and the contrary animals pulled into line. Brody had also chosen mules. Sara looked at her lapel watch. Thirty minutes to starting time.

As Lucas rode past her, checking wagons, ties and any other last-minute details, Sara saw the black-and-blue line along his jaw line. He also had a personal interest in winning this race. As ferocious as the fight had been, it was a wonder neither man had a broken limb or two. She'd caught sight of Brody earlier. He showed no signs of the scuffle.

The crowd quieted as the mule skinners, whips at their sides, began mounting their saddle mule, the last one on the left. Sara clutched her throat. It was all she could do to stand still. She made a quick count of the men. Her heart skipped a beat. She'd only counted thirty, not including Lucas.

She tried again.

This time she included Lucas, the twenty-five drivers and the assistant wagon master. The five guards were with the extra mules. She'd added an extra guard on just to be safe. They not only guarded the stock, they replaced anyone who became sick or killed by Indians, or a deserter who felt the work was too hard.

She could not afford to be short of men.

But that only added up to thirty-two. She glanced around and finally located the two herders and the two night herders off to themselves. Everything was as it should be.

Sara checked her watch again. It was six. She shoved her hands in her wide pockets and like the others, waited.

A gun went off.

"Stretch out!" bellowed Lucas.

The drivers snapped their long whips and swore at

the unruly mules, bidding goodbye to old friends between the oaths. The mules leaned into their collars
and the wagons creaked and groaned as they lurched
forward.

Cheers filled the air. Sara could do nothing now but
wait. She looked across the street at Brody's big brick
building. On the second floor, he stood by a window,
smoking a cigar. What was he thinking while he
waited?

Two days later, one of Sara's men showed her a
wanted poster. Brody was offering one thousand dollars for delivery of Blacky or Odeon Beckman alive.
Below it gave their descriptions. Sara had heard that
Odeon's first job with Hawkins and Associates had
been on the wagons that had been attacked, which
gave Brody even more reason for revenge. It would
appear the killings had been carefully planned.

Sara had turned into a nervous wreck. After two
weeks, and at an approximate average of 125 miles
per week, the outfit had only traveled somewhere
around two hundred and fifty miles of the eight-
hundred-mile stretch!

Hours were spent thinking about the dangers the
wagons would face as they crossed what was called
the Great American Desert. She'd been told about the
stretches of alkali dust that could reach depths of six
inches; the sucking mud; the bitter extremes of hot and

cold; the swollen rivers; and last but certainly not least, the possibility of having to fight unfriendly Indians.

But contrary to what the name implied, there were pockets of settlements in the Great American Desert. Stops would be made to deliver seventy-five tons of food, animal feed, woolens, cotton, silk, suspenders, razors, pocketknives, whiskey, beads, shoes, tools, implements and machinery...everything it took to keep a community growing for another year. All time-consuming.

As paranoia began replacing common sense, Sara asked her other wagon masters what would be the most likely scenario that could cause Lucas to lose the race. Terrain, Indians, stock, illness or weather? It was the consensus that the loss of mules would probably be the most likely problem.

What with summer's end and stock and wagons being put in storage, Sara spent a lot of time taking Buckets out on long rides, even though she knew she should be taking orders for next year's deliveries. On the other hand, it had cost her a considerable amount of money to outfit the wagons, and if she lost the race there wouldn't be any reason to think about next year. She had been a fool to have even made such a ridiculous wager. Her temper was her downfall.

Thoughts of Brody made Sara think even harder of a way of making sure her outfit arrived in Santa Fe first. She finally concluded that she could not stand

back and do nothing. For all she knew, Brody could
be doing all sorts of things to make sure he won the
wager. He could send out more men to help with the
unloading, or have teams of men ready to relieve the
others. Maybe he even had way stations to change
mule teams. He not only had the money, but he was
just underhanded enough to pull such a stunt…no matter what the other freighters said about his honesty.

Though Sara and Brody had agreed to have Hamish
and a man of Brody's choice in Sante Fe to witness
the end of the race, Sara knew that if it hadn't been
for Brody's determination to find out what had happened to his crew, he'd already be headed for Santa
Fe. There was nothing keeping her from doing the
same thing. She deliberated over the clause stating
owners could not travel with the wagons, which she'd
had inserted. Sara decided that there would be no in-
fraction of the contract if she were to deliver extra
mules on her way to Sante Fe. Just how she could
accomplish this was another matter.

Brody sat silently watching the nooses being slipped
over the two men's necks.

"I'm innocent," Blacky protested, tears already
streaming down his ruddy cheeks.

"You can't do this," Odeon yelled. He yanked at
the rope keeping his hands bound behind his back.

Brody glanced around at the open field. "I don't
see anyone stopping me. All I have to do is have my

men release your horses and give them a hard swat on the rear, and you'll be hanging by your neck. You may not die immediately, so in that case I'll be merciful. I'll have you cut down and we'll do it all over again.''

"No-o," Blacky yelled. "I only did what I was told!"

"I hear you're a fair man, Hawkins," Odeon blurted out. "Surely you ain't gonna hang innocent men."

"Turn the horses loose," Brody ordered.

"No! Wait!" Odeon begged, his face white with fear.

"I'm through waiting. Who killed my men?"

"Ok. I'll tell you everything. Just take the noose off me."

Brody nodded his head, and his men removed the ropes. The minute he was free, Odeon planted his heels in his horse's ribs, sending the animal leaping forward in a full gallop. With calm deliberation, Brody pulled his pistol and fired, hitting the bearded man in the shoulder and knocking him out of the saddle.

Two of the five bullwhackers ran forward, yanking a screaming Odeon onto his feet. Another leaped on his horse and took off after the runaway horse.

Brody looked at Blacky who hadn't moved an inch, his face twisted in fear. "What did you mean when you said you did as you were told?"

"I swear, I only told the lady what I was paid to tell her," he said as fast as he could get the words out.

"What lady?"

"The one that owns Miles Freighting." Blacky nervously looked up at the noose still wrapped over a thick branch.

"Who paid you?"

Blacky looked at Odeon being dragged back to the tree. "Odeon. I swear, Mr. Hawkins, I didn't know nothin' except what I was told to tell the lady."

Brody swung his leg over the cantle and stared at the pox-faced man. "Are you saying that the woman and Lucas Collier knew nothing except what you told them?"

"That's what I'm sayin'."

"Kinderman," Brody called to the man holding Blacky's horse, "cut him loose." Brody watched the bullwhacker pull his knife. "Don't try leaving town, Blacky," Brody said as the small man's hands were freed, "not until I get to the bottom of this. If you do, you're a dead man. Now get out of here."

Blacky slowly took hold of the reins, unable to believe his good fortune. "If I learn anything more, I'll let you know."

"You do that."

Blacky nudged his horse forward. Deciding he wasn't going to be shot in the back, he gave his mount a quick kick in the ribs.

Brody put his leg down then dismounted. He walked to where Odeon had been dragged and gave the bearded man a hard shove on his wounded shoulder.

"You're hurting me," Odeon hollered in pain.

"You've only just begun to know what pain is. I'll hang you and cut you down so many times you'll be begging me to get it over with. Twenty-five of my men were murdered, something that makes me mad as hell. After putting the loose ends together, it's become apparent to me that the killing had to be done by the other men, which is why they were never found. And the murders took place after Sara Miles sent her team out to get the wagons. A well-laid plan that took time and lots of money to get men to agree to murder. Someone was behind this. I want to know who that someone is."

Brody stormed into the Riggs's home, not bothering to knock or wait to be escorted in by a servant. "Patricia!" he bellowed.

"Patricia is gone."

Brody turned to see Clara standing in the doorway of the parlor. She looked smaller and older than he'd ever seen her. "Where is Patricia?" he demanded, his words clipped and his impatience showing.

"You found out about Patricia, didn't you?"

"You know?"

"Yes. I live here now, and I've been expecting you." She turned and walked back into the parlor.

"Where is she, Clara?" He followed her into the room.

She pulled the cord for the maid before sitting on a Queen Anne chair. "I've made sure you won't find her."

"She cold-bloodedly had twenty-five of my men killed."

"I know, and it's unforgivable."

"Where is Casey?"

"Sit down Brody, we have to talk."

"I have nothing to say."

"I know you're impatient, but surely you can humor an old lady."

Brody hesitated, then took a seat on the sofa. "Why did she do it, Clara?"

Clara looked at the handsome, unforgiving face of a man she truly respected. So tall and powerful and determined. She couldn't blame him for wanting revenge. She'd feel the same were she in his shoes. She glanced down at her shaking hands, then held them up for Brody to see. "Age is taking its toll, Brody. Even a month ago I could walk steadier than I can now."

The maid entered and went straight to Clara. "Can I do something for you, ma'am?"

"Yes. Bring the decanter of my son's best whiskey and two glasses."

The maid hurried over to the sideboard. "Shall I pour the drinks?" she asked as she set the articles on a table in front of Clara.

"No, that will be all. Leave us alone now and close the doors behind you."

After the tall, sliding doors had been shut, Clara poured two drinks then handed one to Brody. She took a long sip, appreciating the flavor. "You know, I had such hopes that you would fall in love with Sara. She's such a sweet child."

"I don't care to discuss Sara. I want to know where Patricia and Casey are."

"But this involves Sara. As for my son, he had nothing to do with any of this. He's as badly shaken up as you are. Probably even more so."

Brody downed his drink. "What are you trying to tell me, Clara?"

Clara finished her drink and offered Brody another. He shook his head. She poured herself one. "As one gets older, we come to realize that not all things have completion. Sometimes we have to be content with the medium."

"Are you saying that Patricia isn't going to pay for her crimes?"

"Not the way you would have it. I also have contacts, Brody, and when Sara told me what had happened I started doing some snooping. Fortunately I came by my information before you did. Then it was a simple matter of confronting Patricia with the truth. She tried denying all accusations, but the proof left her helpless. As much as I have always disliked Patricia, I could not allow the mother of my grandsons to be hung in a public square. The boys would carry her guilt for the rest of their lives.''

Clara caught her breath. ''Patricia will pay for her crime, Brody, but in a different way. I wanted to be sure you couldn't track her down, so, after signing divorce papers, she was taken to another town then handed a stagecoach ticket west and enough money to get her there. For once in her life she'll have to find a way to survive. She won't return for fear of being hung.''

Clara sipped her whiskey to wet her dry throat. ''Casey wanted to be the one to tell you everything, but I insisted on doing it. I knew the truth would eventually have to be told, but I wanted Patricia gone before it happened.''

Brody stood and refilled his glass. He downed the contents in one gulp. ''And is she gone?''

''Yes.''

''Did she tell you why she did all this?''

''She wanted to be the only woman in your life. She said she would have gladly left Casey if you asked her to.''

Brody raked his fingers through his thick hair.

''Patricia had gone so far as to hire a housekeeper for Sara so she could keep tabs on the time you spent with Sara. But when Sara fired the housekeeper, Patricia was left high and dry. I'm sure she did other things to prevent the two of you from being together, but we'll never know what they were, nor is there any reason to know. The attack on your wagons was a desperate effort to close Sara down and make her leave town.''

Brody's jaw muscled twitched. ''And she knew we were going to be gone when it happened.'' He set the empty glass down then walked to the tall doors. ''Tell Casey I'll talk to him in a couple of weeks. It'll give us both time to settle down some. In the meantime, I see no reason for others to know what's happened.'' He slid the doors open and left.

For the following two weeks, Brody stayed away from the men's club and remained alone as much as possible. He wasn't finding it easy to come to terms with himself. He thought about how cleverly Clara had tied his hands. There was nothing more he could do about the unjust killings. He knew the names of the men who'd taken part in the slaughter and they would pay for their crimes.

Brody considered himself partly to blame for what had happened. He and Patricia had had a brief affair some years back, which she had put an end to. He knew she wanted him back in her bed, but he hadn't realized to what extremes she was willing to go to get him there. And then there was Sara. Like it or not, eventually he was going to have to eat humble pie. That she would make it easy on him wasn't even a remote possibility.

Deciding to get it over and done with, Brody once

again made his way across the busy street. Not seeing her buggy parked in her usual spot, he assumed she was gone.

When Brody stepped inside the Miles Freighting building, he didn't recognize a single man. For a brief moment, he hesitated, wondering if he had entered the wrong door.

"May I help you, sir?" the older man inquired.

"I'm here to see Miss Miles. "

"She's not in today. May I help you with something?"

"No, I need to talk to her privately. Will she be in later?"

"Oh, no, sir. Miss Miles is on her way to Santa Fe with her mules and she won't be back—"

"Son of a bitch!"

"I beg your—" The gentleman had left before Mr. Hackett had a chance to finished his protest.

Chapter Twenty

The dawn had awakened with streaks of pink, yellow and orange as Sara and the three men rode away from the Last Chance Store, aptly named. It was the last opportunity to replenish supplies, make repairs or find wood and a timely stop for wagon trains. For the last time, Sara was asked if she wanted to turn back. She'd stubbornly refused.

Sara pulled her floppy hat down firmly on her head then turned in the saddle to check the ten mules following in single file, the lead rope wrapped around her gloved hand. Satisfied she looked ahead at Joe, Buck and Mack, each leading another ten mules. Sara had firmly convinced herself that the forty ornery animals were exactly what would take Lucas and her outfit to victory.

The first few nights of the trail, Sara had been too miserable and too tired to get a good night's rest, which made the next day even more miserable. Her legs, back and shoulders protested and the hard ground she had to sleep on aggravated an already bad situation. But no matter what the pain, not once did she complain. She couldn't. The men she'd hired had already let her know that they considered her plan to be foolhardy.

Though it was the beginning of fall, the weather had remained hot, the blue sky devoid of clouds, and the scorched land was in desperate need of rain. Even the tall buffalo grass that reached as high as the horses' underbellies had turned golden in color. Sara constantly wiped the perspiration from her forehead. At least she'd finally accepted the wisdom of the clothing worn by women who worked on outfits and had exchanged her skirts for the pair of jeans she'd purchased at the Last Chance Store. She'd added rawhide chaps simply because her men wore them.

The three men Sara had hired had traveled the Santa Fe Trail many times. They were older and looked as if they hadn't bathed or shaved in years, but her papa had always said they were trustworthy and honest. Since Sara had never traveled the Trail before, their experience was invaluable.

The foursome rode from dawn to sunset, stopping only for a quick meal at high noon. The travel was demanding, and the men were kind enough not to talk about the times they had to slow down because of Sara. They weren't traveling as fast as she wanted because the horses and mules often needed to be kept at a slow pace so they wouldn't become overheated, and the terrain was not always flat and easily traversed.

At times Sara was convinced she couldn't go another mile. But slowly her endurance grew and the sore muscles became stronger. After almost two weeks, she could actually keep up with the others, an accomplishment she was quite proud of.

As her physical condition improved, Sara became even more obsessed with the importance of getting the mules to Lucas. Buck had estimated that at the rate they were traveling, they'd reach Lucas about three-quarters of the way, or possibly a little farther, depending on how fast Lucas had the outfit moving.

They were all weary and thirsty by the time they reached the Diamond of the Plain. Sara had never seen anything as welcoming as the clear, cold, natural spring. She had learned that good water was a rare treat on the Trail. Though still needing to push on, they spent the day letting the animals graze and rest, as well as themselves. Sara even found a spot where she could bathe privately. Once clean, she was rejuvenated. Just before dawn, they again moved on.

They had traveled another a 105 miles when the trail crossed a series of small streams, cutting the prairie from north to south, each one more difficult to cross than the last. The creeks were narrow with steep, muddy banks. As hard as Sara tried, she could not get her ten belligerent mules up and over the sides. The men had to take their stock across, then one of them would return to take hers.

Sara no longer thought of streams as places to bathe. Being covered with trail dust had become a way of life and trying to stay clean was a losing battle.

When they reached the Old Stone Corral, Sara insisted the mules be turned loose and free to roam about. The area was huge, but completely enclosed by a tall rock wall. The others were against releasing them, saying they'd have a hell of a time catching them and getting them tied back onto the lines. Sara ignored their words of wisdom and accused them of acting like a bunch of women.

The following morning, Sara ate her words. After a breakfast consisting of bacon and coffee, the men set out to catch the mules. Five hours later, they rode on. Considering the men's disposition, Sara knew the wisest course would be for her to keep her mouth shut and not even try offering an apology.

Past Turkey Creek, the land turned harsh. Mack warned Sara of tumblebugs and rattlesnakes. Sara had never liked snakes of any kind and most certainly not rattlers. The farther west they traveled the more obvious evidence of hard times became. Bleached bones of long-dead bison were seen, and what were once flowing streams were now nothing but dry, cracked earth. Even buffalo couldn't find water in the barren land.

Though Sara thought she had already been through

the worst of the trip, the discomforts were only beginning. Many days followed that her throat stayed parched and her cracked lips begged for a drop of water. But the men were having the same problems, and water had to be rationed. Meanwhile, the unrelenting sun continued to beat down on them.

One night after supper, the men explained to Sara that they were about to enter the Great Plains area, which was the land of the buffalo and hostile Indian country. The area stretched from Pawnee Rock to the Cimarron crossing and it was necessary that they keep a constant vigil. Raiding had become a way of life for the Comanches and with only three men and one woman, they were extremely vulnerable.

It was also time to decide which route to take. The longer one, which meant following the river and watching for Indians, or the shorter mountain route? The men agreed that since they were traveling much faster than the wagons, the longer route would be preferable because of the water. Due to the time of the year, the shorter route meant possible snowstorms.

For Sara, the prairie she had always heard about suddenly opened up. She would never have believed there were so many buffalo had she not seen it with her own eyes. Huge herds were constantly in sight, and the land seemingly stretched out forever.

It was midafternoon when, seemingly out of nowhere, a storm struck. Long streaks of lightning struck the ground and the claps of thunder were nonstop, terrifying Sara as well as the herd of buffalo they had been circling. Then a deafening clap of thunder hit practically overhead, setting the buffalo into a stampede. Blinded by sudden shields of rain, Sara heard the rumbling of hooves as the big beasts raced forward, but fear had caused indecision. Buckets reared and the mules began kicking, eager to escape the oncoming slaughter.

For a brief moment before the sky had opened up, Sara thought she'd seen Brody. In her panicked state she had to have been hallucinating. She couldn't even see the faces of the two riders who had come for her, one taking the mules, the other grabbing the side of her reins and sending the two horses racing from the oncoming herd.

As suddenly as the terrible thunderstorm came, it went away. Even the buffalo had slowed down, some grazing again. Drenched to the bone, as soon as the horses were brought to a halt, Sara turned to thank her rescuer.

"Brody!"

"That's right, Brody," he mimicked. "I still find it hard to believe you would pull something like this," he snapped at her. "You came very close to getting yourself killed, lady."

"You weren't concerned about my safety." She snatched her reins from his hand. "You're here to keep me from delivering these mules to Lucas and thereby winning the race. Well, it's not going to work."

"You're so obsessed with the race you can't even think straight."

"You tell your Indian friend I want those mules back, then you can leave. I never want to set eyes on you again, at least not until you pay me my winnings."

The Indian rode up and handed her the lead. Satisfied, Sara nudged Buckets forward to where her men were waiting. It galled her the way they greeted Brody. They all dismounted and shook hands, as if he were some long-lost friend.

"You been lookin' for us?" Joe asked, a big smile spread across his face.

"Yep," Brody replied. He pulled off his wet duster and slung it over the saddle.

"I always said Felaytay was the best damn tracker there was," Buck commented as he shoved a wad of tobacco inside his cheek.

They all know each other, Sara thought with a shock.

"Why the hell would the three of you agree to go along with this foolhardy notion?" Brody asked.

Mack shook his bushy head and chuckled. "It was either that or let her hire some crooks who'd end up takin' her mules and killin' her. We knowed her pa. He was a good man."

Sara seethed with indignation. "Are we moving on

or are we going to spend the time gabbing like a bunch of women?''

The men looked at the woman still primly seated atop her horse. "We need to stop and dry out, ma'am."

"Fine. There's still several hours of daylight left, so if you'll hand me the lead ropes I'll go on without you."

The three men turned to Brody, as if waiting for him to find an agreeable solution.

Brody shoved his hat to the back of his head, tucked his thumbs under his gun belt and looked at the stubborn woman. "And just where are you going, Sara?"

"You know where I'm going," she snapped at him.

"I didn't realize you were familiar with the trail."

After all the hard terrain she'd covered, the unpredictable weather, thirst and a dozen other things she didn't care to think about, for Brody to show up out of nowhere and act as if he were the boss was more than Sara could take. She slowly dismounted, taking her whip with her. Before Brody had time to figure out what she was up to, she'd uncoiled the seven feet of braided rawhide.

Joe was the first to see what was about to happen. "Now, ma'am," he said placing his hand palm out to her, "ain't no need for you to go getting' riled. The storm got us all drenched."

The others turned and faced her.

"I hired you men, and I'm paying you. You work for me, not that no-account. Brody, get out of here."

Brody pursed his lips as he studied the woman, feet

spread and both hands grasping the handle of the bull-whip. Even if the colonel hadn't told him she knew how to use it, her stance was all the evidence he needed. "You know, Sara, you're forcing me to take that away from you." He watched Felaytay moving around behind her.

In one quick motion, Sara flipped the whip, the loud, cracking sound echoing in the still air. When the end fell back to the ground, Brody had one less button on his shirt.

Brody's fury uncoiled as he assessed the situation. "Lady, I have had my fill of your threats. First it was a gun, now a whip."

The next lash was to his pistol, pulling it from his holster and dropping it to the ground. "I said leave."

Joe, Buck and Mack kept looking from Sara to Brody, not sure what they should do.

Even though Felaytay had drawn closer to her, Brody waited until she raised the whip again, this time nipping at the toe of his boots. The whip was long and heavy, and before she could raise it again, he charged forward and yanked the handle from her grasp. She tried to slap him, but he easily caught her wrist, holding it in midair. "Sara, dear, I'm going to say this one time, and one time only."

Sara sneered at him.

"The next time you try pulling something like this, I guarantee I will put you over my lap and give you the hardest spanking of you life. Felaytay and I have already spotted several Indian bands in the area, just looking for something as sweet as you and your mules. It was only a matter of time before you were seen and attacked. But if we're lucky, I'm going to get us out of here alive.''

Brody released her wrist then picked up the whip and tossed it to his friend, Felaytay. ''Make sure she doesn't get her hands on it again, and check to see if she has a pistol hidden in her saddlebags. After that, ride out and see if there are any renegades in the near vicinity. Meanwhile, we'll try to get dried out.''

Felaytay nodded and silently moved away.

Sara stood watching Joe and Mack take care of the mules while Buck stripped the supply packs and un-saddled the horses. They all avoided eye contact. Sara wanted to strangle every one of them. It had been bad enough for Brody to have humiliated her in front of her own men, but for them to act as if nothing had happened instead of coming to her rescue would make any one furious. Furthermore, there was little doubt in her mind that Brody had deliberately made up the story about seeing Indians.

Left with no alternative but to stay with the others, and with her wet clothes starting to itch, Sara reached under Buckets's belly and undid the cinch. The sun was bright again and it shouldn't take long for things to dry out.

She pulled off the saddle and blanket and laid them out in the tall grass. After giving Buckets a quick rub-down, she turned the mare loose, knowing she wouldn't stray far. Cursing under her breath, Sara snatched up her saddlebags and proceeded to wade through the tall, wet grass. Thick swarms of biting gnats were suddenly everywhere and she had to keep brushing them from her face.

After going far enough not to be seen, Sara quickly pulled dry clothes from her saddlebags and changed. She hurried back to the others where the gnats weren't quite so bad.

"Here." Brody shoved a rawhide bag it her. "Put it on your face and hands. It'll help."

Sara was tempted to throw it in his face, but the bugs were intolerable. Inside the bag was a chalky type substance that stank badly, but once applied the gnats left her alone. Under no circumstance would she thank Brody for his help.

Hearing several crows cawing overhead, Sara looked up. It was amazing how the sky looked so peaceful as did the prairie. A deceiving land that was burning hot or freezing cold; a place where thunderstorms came out of nowhere and left as quickly; a heaven for carnivorous gnats lived; and home to Indians who were busy looking for scalps.

No fires were lit that night for fear of attracting Indians and dinner consisted of hardtack and dried buffalo meat. Everyone went to bed early, but for the first time in days, Sara had difficulty falling asleep. Besides still being furious at Brody, she worried about getting the mules to Lucas. She desperately needed a way to get rid of Brody. She still had her rifle, but she could never shoot anyone in cold blood. Besides, he'd only end up taking it away from her.

Two days passed and Sara and Brody hadn't spoken a word to one other. They were now traveling at a slower pace because Brody wanted as little dust kicked into the air as possible. Sara finally had to admit there was nothing she could do about her predicament. She'd have to wait until they reached Fort Mann-Atkinson. If for some unforeseen reason Lucas had already passed through, she could possibly sell the mules for the two hundred dollars a pair she paid for them.

It was late afternoon when Felaytay came galloping his horse toward them, waving his arms.

"Trouble," Brody uttered as he brought the group to a halt.

Brody's friend rode up and said something to Brody, then pointed off to the right.

"A band of Comanches are just over the ridge," Brody repeated. "Make for that passage between those red rocks as fast as you can. Hopefully we can get in there before being seen."

Sara and the others whipped their horses into a gallop.

Chapter Twenty-One

Sara walked to the front of the cave. How much longer would it take for a beam of daylight to show its face? How many hours had she spent reliving the past, wanting to hold it close, for fear she and Brody would not be sharing a future?

Sara walked around the dark cave stretching, trying to rid the kinks in her muscles from sitting so long. She adjusted the bandanna she'd placed over her nose earlier. With the night's cold the cave had become damp and the rancid stench overwhelming. The bandanna helped some, but not much.

For the hundredth time Sara looked out the mouth of the cave, praying she'd see something...anything. Several hours ago the circle of fire had died and now there was nothing but a black void and maddening silence. She had no idea as to Brody's whereabouts, or if he still lived.

Sara flopped down on her bedroll, knowing that in

minutes she'd be back on her feet. With Brody suffering below, any form of rest was impossible. After hours of waiting, unable to help Brody, her stomach felt like she'd been eating thorny cactus.

Something caught her eye. Had she just seen a tiny ray of light flash across the top of the cave? She leaped to her feet and ran to the opening. Yes! The sky was much lighter and rays of sun were coming from behind the rocks. She looked below. It was still cloaked in darkness. Almost afraid to breathe, she waited.

Dark images began to take shape. She rubbed her eyes, trying to get a clearer view. What she first saw left her stunned. Buckets stood alone, barebacked, her reins dragging the ground. At last Sara could see the top of the pole. Tears streaked her face. Brody was no longer tied to it. The Indians had taken him. She sank to her knees sobbing, wishing they had taken her as well.

Through her tears, Sara watched sunlight wash over the valley floor. It took several moments before she realized someone was lying at the base of the pole! She started to charge out of the cave, but caught herself. Was this a trick? She couldn't see the man's face. She yanked off her bandanna and wiped her eyes.

Carefully Sara scanned the area, taking in every rock, gully and boulder. Seeing nothing, she cautiously stepped out of the cave for a better view. Still nothing. If the renegades were hiding, surely she'd spot them from this height. And Buckets was standing peacefully. Only her long tail swished occasionally to ward off flies. Then Sara saw shadows. Buzzards were circling above.

Sara tore back into the cave, tossed the reins over the buckskin's neck and leaped into the saddle. With one hard kick she sent the horse out of the cave and down the rocky path, oblivious of the danger. All Sara could think about was getting to Brody.

Buckets shied away as Sara rode up. Cautiously she dismounted, continually looking over her shoulder to see if anyone would attack. The naked man lay in a fetal position, turned toward the ground, an arm covering the side of his face. Then Sara saw the scar on the back, the one Brody had once told her had come from a bullet wound.

Sara dropped to her knees. Was he dead? Slowly, carefully she moved the arm. Hearing him groan was like being spoken to by the gods. Tears of joy rolled down her cheeks. Brody was unconscious, but alive.

Sara chewed at her bottom lip, trying to get control of her emotions. She looked around, assessing their situation. They were in the middle of nowhere without water or food, and Brody was running a fever. She had always bragged that she was perfectly capable of taking care of herself and the time had come to prove it. Unfortunately she hadn't an inkling as to how they were going to get out of this.

Sara approached the most obvious problem first. Brody had to have shade. The cave was too high up

and too far, but there were no trees and If he remained
here, the blistering sun would surely kill him. Again
she looked around, this time searching along the bottom of the boulder formations. Finally she spotted a
recess. It wasn't a cave, but it dipped in far enough to
make a good shelter. But how would she get him
there? He was far too heavy to lift. Her bedroll! By
the time she'd collected the bedroll from the cave,
Sara knew what she had to do. She squeezed her eyes
shut then opened them, gaining strength for the task
ahead. She thanked God that Brody was unconscious.

It took every bit of strength Sara could muster to
roll Brody on top of her bedroll with his arms resting
on his stomach. After releasing the rope from the side
of her saddle, looping the rope over Brody's head,
bedroll and under his arms was equally difficult. Fortunately the bedroll would give padding as well as
protection. Even so, she had to tell herself over and
over that it had to be done if she was to save him.

Lastly, Sara wrapped the rope around the saddle
horn. Taking the buckskin's reins, she led the gelding
as slowly as possible, dragging Brody behind. She'd
die before she'd let him become the sun's victim or
the vultures' meal.

Once Sara had Brody in front of the recessed rock,
she had to drag him inside to the shade, inch by inch,
her arms screaming with pain. She needed water
badly, but there was little left in her canteen.

Satisfied that Brody was as safe as she could make

him, Sara slipped off Buckets's bridle then mounted
the buckskin. She didn't like leaving Brody alone, but
she had to find water. When she rode off, Buckets
followed.

Sara hadn't gone far when she saw buzzards on the
ground, pecking away at something. Curious, Sara
drew her horse closer. She recognized the three men's
clothing and had a peek at their faceless forms before
sinking her heels in the gelding's ribs. The men had
been scalped.

Frantic, Sara rode off with the gelding in a full gallop. She hadn't gone far before again bringing the
horse to a halt. She dismounted and leaned over just
in time to throw up. Time and again Sara heaved, even
after there was nothing left in her stomach. She
couldn't rid her mind of the three men she'd seen only
minutes ago.

Shaking and her face devoid of color, Sara finally
climbed back in the saddle. She still had to locate water, and nothing she could do would reverse what had
happened. She hadn't gone far when she came upon
Brody's Indian friend. He'd been buried up to the neck
and ants were still crawling over what was left of his
head. Never in her life had she hated any one or thing
as she did now. But the one she should hate most was
herself. She'd been the cause of all of this and she'd
bear guilt for the rest of her life. They had been good
men.

Ten minutes later and still shaking badly, Sara spotted Brody's saddle, saddlebags, canteens, bedroll and even his duster. She couldn't come up with a single reason as to why the items had been discarded. At least Brody would have clothes to keep him warm.

After nearly an hour of searching rocky outcrops for water, Sara was ready to give up. Buckets suddenly pricked her ears forward and galloped off in a different direction. Curious, Sara followed. The mare had smelled water and had headed straight for it. It was a small stream trailing between the rocks. One of the boulders had a good-size dip in it, allowing a pool to form before the sweet water continued on. The horses and Sara drank their fill before returning to where she'd left Brody. As it turned out, the water was quite near.

Sara changed her mind about trying to dress Brody. His hind side was chaffed from being dragged and his chest wound and others were open. She ended up placing the clothes on top of him. There was nothing she could do about the bruises covering his body, but she did a fairly good job of cleaning the lacerations. The Indians hadn't been kind to him.

For three days and nights, Sara put wet compresses on Brody's head, trying to break the fever. She built a small fire with buffalo chips and heated water in the small skillet that was part of her pack. Jerky and hardtack were added to make soup. Each day she carefully forced some of it down Brody's throat. More than once she silently thanked Indian Bob for the things he'd patiently taught her.

She spoke to Brody as she nursed him. "Do you hear me, Brody Hawkins?" she'd ask. "If you die I'll never forgive you!"

Other times she'd talk to him about her papa and brother, even though she knew he couldn't hear her. In between, she collected various scrub bushes and managed to form a makeshift brace for Brody's arm. Strips of cloth from a petticoat were used to bind it.

The nights were the worst for Sara. Nightmares of mutilated men plagued her and she'd wake up in a cold sweat. Then she'd lay awake for hours, afraid to go to sleep again. The wind brought sounds of coyote cries and one night she heard Indian war whoops in the distance. Last night she'd stood outside the temporary shelter and stared up at the millions of stars. She'd felt as if she were standing in the middle of them. A shooting star had shot through the sky, and she'd made a wish. Maybe it would help Brody get well.

On the morning of the fourth day, Brody's fever had broken and for the first time he rested peacefully. That afternoon he opened his eyes, once again ready to face the world. But when he tried to sit up, he discovered how weak he'd become and his arm hurt like hell. He did, however, drink nearly a cup of her soup before dropping off to sleep.

"Brody," Sara said late that night, "do you feel like telling me why the Indians let you live?"

"I challenged the head man to a fight. I won and told him I had taken his coup."

"What's a coup?"

"When a man is killed, the Indian believes he takes that man's bravery and strength, and it becomes his own. It's referred to as 'counting coup.' Touching an enemy with the bare hand or other brave deeds is the same thing. I had told the brave that his strengths were now mine. He was determined to prove I didn't have his coup by torturing me. Another brave became angry and said I had proven my right to live."

Brody winced as he moved his bad arm. "The renegades began arguing among themselves over the matter. It was finally decided to leave me a horse, and they'd let the gods decided if I should live or die. I told them Buckets was my horse." The effort to speak wore him out and soon he was sound asleep.

Sara wondered if the Indian who had been on his side had deliberately left the saddle and his things. They'd never know.

The next morning Brody felt considerably better. "I sent Felaytay to the fort for help," he informed Sara. "I'm surprised they haven't already arrived."

"He didn't make it," Sara said sadly.

"He's dead?"

Sara nodded. Brody remained silent the rest of the morning.

Knowing she could wait no longer, Sara informed Brody that tomorrow she would ride to Fort Atkinson for help. "There are only a few strips of jerky left," she said that afternoon. "When that's gone we'll have nothing to eat."

He was lying on his back with his eyes closed. "I said—"

"I heard you. We'll leave first thing in the morning."

"Oh, no," Sara stated. "You're in no condition to travel."

"I said we'll leave in the morning."

Sara banged the pan down on the ground and leaped to her feet. "I don't care what you said. Do you think that after all I've been through to keep you alive that I'm going to watch you die on the trail? You don't even have the strength to climb on a horse. You need proper food to regain—"

"What do you care if I live or die? If I remember correctly, the last time we talked you wanted nothing more to do with me except to receive your money if I lost our wager."

"Well, you certainly took care of that by getting rid of my mules."

Brody propped his back against the rock then, ignoring the sharp pain, carefully shifting his broken arm to a more comfortable position. "Now that you've brought up the subject, just what possessed you to take off on such a stupid journey?"

"I wanted to be sure I didn't lose everything to you," Sara defended.

"You know as well as I do that it takes three hundred mules to pull a twenty-five wagon outfit, plus all the extra ones," he snapped at her. "How, may I ask, did you expect forty to make a difference?"

"That's my business," she retorted as she left the protection of the alcove.

"You mean you were so obsessed with the possibility of losing that you never gave it proper thought," Brody yelled after her.

Sara stomped back in, hands on hips, brown eyes as black as pitch. "Why didn't you finish? Why didn't you say that because of my actions four good men are now dead, and you have possibly lost the use of your arm?"

Brody shook his head. "It would figure that you now want to take on the responsibility for their deaths," he said harshly. "Are you so almighty that you could have predicted what would happen?"

"No. I—"

"The prairie is wild and unpredictable. Many have crossed it and never once laid eyes on a single Indian. You didn't put those renegades at the very place and time we arrived, Sara. Luck just wasn't with us. Mac, Joe and Buck agreed to come with you, knowing the dangers they might have to face. Their lives were not your responsibility."

Brody wiggled around and laid back down on the

bedroll, his back turned to Sara. "How did you plan on finding the fort? You don't even know the way. Now get some sleep. We'll leave early in the morning while it's still cool."

Sara wanted to continue the argument, but in her heart, she knew that any further protest would be wasted words. Besides, how had she planned to reach the fort when she didn't even know its location?

"Sara," he said in a sleepy voice, "I know you weren't behind having my wagons waylaid."

Sara stared at his back. "Did you find out who did it?"

"Yes, and they're paying their dues."

Dumbfounded, Sara waited for a further explanation, but none was forthcoming. Instead she heard Brody softly snoring. She wanted to know who had caused her to wager her business. How could he fall asleep without explaining how he knew she was innocent and who was behind the murders of his men? She had a right to know!

Sara fetched her bedroll and rolled it out. After making herself as comfortable as possible, she lay with her eyes wide-open. It had hurt deeply when Brody accused her of murder. Suddenly he'd blurted out that he knew she was innocent and even had the nerve to act as if it were of little importance. How could he be so callous?

But the other things Brody had said had her thinking. It wasn't likely he'd been trying to make her feel better, but what he'd said about the four men had relieved the guilt from already heavy shoulders.

And the part about the ridiculousness of her attempt to save her business with a paltry forty mules had opened something in her brain. What *had* she expected to accomplish?

Her thoughts drifted back to when she'd first come up with the idea of taking mules to Lucas. Everyone had tried to talk her out of it, but totally convinced she was going to save her company, she'd ignored anything said to her.

Everything seemed so clear to Sara now. She took a deep breath then slowly let the air back out. Unfortunately the truth had arrived too late to save the four dead men.

Sara was up before dawn, and by the time Brody awoke she already had the canteens filled with water and the horses saddled. She fixed them both a cup of coffee with the ground beans she'd been saving and followed that with the last of the prepared soup.

After tucking everything in one of the saddlebags, she slung it behind the saddle. Now she and Brody, who had somehow managed to stand, would attempt to dress him. The dressing went smoother than Sara had thought, but she knew having clothes touching his cuts couldn't be comfortable. Holding on to the pommel with his good hand, he easily swung his leg over the buckskin's rump and mounted him. When his bronzed face paled, she knew his arm was hurting, and probably everything else. Sara crossed her fingers. So far, so good.

Brody led the way and Sara followed, her rifle stuffed in the scabbard. Because of Brody's condition, they had to travel slowly. But if Brody was right and there were no further interruptions, it would only take two full days to reach Fort Atkinson.

When the fort came into view, Sara wanted to ride ahead and get the doctor, but she didn't. The only thing that had kept Brody in the saddle was sheer will-power. They had crossed a long stretch of alkali and it had worked its way inside Brody's clothes, making his cuts burn as badly as if a branding iron had been put to him. But he was a proud man and she would not take away his determination to make it to the fort on his own. She still hated him for using her, but her admiration would never change.

The fort was busy with civilians and cavalry soldiers moving from place to place, others just standing about looking at the strangers who had just ridden in.

Sara and Brody rode in silence. He didn't bring his horse to stop until they reached the commander's building. Brody managed to dismount then stood for several seconds, pulling his strength together. Finally he walked up the two steps and entered the wooden building.

Sara dismounted then looped both horses' reins over the hitching post. Before she could follow Brody inside, a private hurried out and took off toward another building. Sara suspected the young man had left to get the doctor. Anyone with half an eye could tell Brody needed help.

Inside, Brody rested on a chair, his face bathed in sweat. The fort commander stood in front of him, listening to Brody tell what had happened. He turned to Sara.

"And you must be Sara Miles," he said, his bushy eyebrows pulled together with concern.

"Yes," she acknowledged.

"From what Hawkins was just telling me, you're a very brave woman. I've sent for the doctor. How Hawkins made it here in his condition is quite unbelievable."

"I agree," she said softly.

"In the meantime, I'll make arrangements for you to stay with the widow Fredrickson. She'll see to it that you get a bath and a good meal."

Sara smiled.

Sara stayed at the fort for several days, resting and eating almost everything she could get her hands on. She didn't visit Brody in the hospital because there was no purpose to it. He belonged to Patricia.

Santa Fe was nothing like Sara had expected. There were narrow, alleylike streets, adobe houses with ladders outside to reach the second floors, and strings of red peppers hung everywhere. Big-eyed children played and dogs constantly barked. At night, lights shone from the busy, noisy dance halls where it seemed to Sara that all men gathered, including Hamish Goodman.

Yet everyone seemed to have a quick smile to offer and though it could be termed a rowdy town, Sara rather liked it. However, if anyone were to ask her why, she wouldn't be able to supply a satisfactory answer.

Every day Sara went to the Wells Fargo office to see if Lucas had sent word ahead of the outfit's arrival, and every day she returned to her hotel room to wait again. Her short stay would have been miserable if Hamish hadn't been there to witness the winning outfit. He was quite happy to show Sara about and quick to point out the areas she should and shouldn't go to. Sara bought clothes and various other items. In fact she bought so much she ended up having to purchase a suitcase to carry them in.

When word did come of Lucas's impending arrival the next day, Sara felt no sense of joy.

It was nearing dusk when Lucas arrived with the wagons. Word of the race had reached Santa Fe, and everyone seemed to have turned out to see the winner. Sara stood off to the side as one wagon after another moved through the town square. Brody's outfit wasn't anywhere in sight.

"See, your mules weren't necessary."

Sara spun around. Brody stood right behind her, tall and as handsome as ever. Other than the sling around his neck to support his broken arm, he looked in perfect health. She wanted to touch him and inquire about his condition, but she didn't. It would seem too personal. She tilted her chin and looked him straight in the eye. "I believe you owe me a good deal of money."

"I'll make sure a note reaches your desk," he replied, his words clipped. "You should be feeling quite excited about keeping your freight company."

Sara looked away. "But was it worth all that happened?" She turned and walked away.

Chapter Twenty-Two

The four men sat in the Bucket of Ale, enjoying their drinks and fine cigars. Casey was still uneasy around the others after what his wife had done, but he and Brody had made their peace. As agreed, no one else knew what had taken place other than that Casey and Patricia had divorced.

"So Hamish stayed in Santa Fe?" Lester mused. "I do believe we're going to miss him popping in now and then."

"He said he preferred the weather," Brody said.

Otis gave Brody a slap on the back. "And you," he chuckled, "not only let a little woman take the fort contracts out from under your nose, you turned right around and let her beat you to Santa Fe by eight hours." He hit the table with his fist and roared with laughter.

The other two joined in, finding it equally funny.

Brody grinned. "She won fair and square. That wagon master, Lucas, is one hell of a man."

"Isn't he the one you got into a fight with?" Otis asked.

Brody nodded. "One in the same."

"I heard about that," Casey said as he stirred his coffee. Liquor only seemed to make his loneliness worse. "I guess the rumors about you being good with your fists were right." He sipped his coffee then set it back down. It was too hot. "The fight must have taken place shortly before our trip to Washington. Before Patricia's talk with Sara?"

Eyes narrowed, Brody took a long draw on his cigar then slowly blew it out. "What talk, Casey?"

Casey's face turned almost as red as his hair. "I have no idea what it was about. It couldn't have been anything important. I'm sorry I mentioned it."

"Tell me, anyway."

"Patricia was late for a supper I was giving for some backers. She apologized saying she'd been visiting with Sara at her office and hadn't realized how much time had slipped by."

"And you said this was before we left for Washington?"

"That's right."

"How long before we left?" Brody took another drag on his cigar.

"I don't remember. Maybe two or three days."

Brody grew silent as the others discussed the possibility of a hard winter. If Patricia had hated Sara so much, why had she paid Sara a visit?

Sara had been sick when she returned to Leavenworth by way of stagecoach. However, after plenty of rest and her housekeeper's good doctoring, she felt great and had been eager to return to work.

The first thing Sara found out was that Brody had not made an appearance to pay his debt, nor had he transferred money into her account. It galled her to think she would have to take him to court to collect, but she refused to let him escape paying off their wager. Thank goodness she'd had enough brain left to insist on a contract.

The next day, Brody sat in Sara's office holding a note in his hand for seventy-five thousand dollars. "I believe I owe you this," he said with a clear voice. He placed it on the desk in front of him and watched Sara take it, making sure the amount was correct.

"I doubt that this left your pockets empty. You'd probably pay this for some horse wager."

Sara had changed. Her silver-blond hair had been pulled straight back into a chignon at the nape. Her face was still darkened by her days in the sun and her long lashes still rimmed a pair of big, brown eyes, but there was an unquestionable look of peace about her. She had faced her demons and had learned to live with them. "I won't be able to turn any business your way until early spring."

"That will be fine." Damn him, he made her feel guilty for thinking he wasn't going to comply with their agreement. His arm was no longer in a sling. Surely it couldn't have healed so soon. She gave way to her curiosity. "Is your arm healed?"

He could smell the perfume he'd become so familiar with. "As it happened, it wasn't broken. Just knocked out of the socket. The doctor put it back in place."

"And your cuts?"

"Another quirk. Though the alkali burned like hell, it actually healed them."

Sara thought of all the work she'd done to keep him alive. "Well, I'm glad to see you're doing better." Sara stood. "Forgive my bad manners, but I would appreciate if you'd leave. I have a multitude of work to do."

"Yes, of course." Brody stood but didn't move. "But before I go, I'd like you to answer a question that's been on my mind for some time."

"What is the question?"

"As I recall, the last time we were together in the hunting cabin, you left upset when I told you Casey and Patricia would be accompanying me to Washington. Then when I returned you said you never wanted to see me again. You said it wasn't because of another man, so perhaps you can now tell me why you ended it between us."

Sara gripped the edge of the desk. "I really don't care to discuss it."

He gave her an ingratiating smile. "Since it has ended between us, surely you can do that one little favor for me."

"If I hadn't ended it, you would have eventually." Sara had tried sounding flippant, but it hadn't come off well.

"I see. And that's all there was to it?"

"Yes."

"Mmm. By the way, your green velvet suit is most attractive." Brody headed for the door and stopped. "Before I leave, there's something I should tell you, but you have to promise you'll never repeat it to another soul."

Sara realized he was waiting for her answer. "I promise."

"I'm telling you only because you were involved. Patricia Riggs was behind the waylaying of my outfit and the killing of my men."

Sara fell back onto the chair, her mouth open.

"She did it because she wanted you out of business and out of town. She's gone now and won't be returning." He took a couple more steps and stopped again. "One other thing. Since I knew your forty mules would gain you nothing, why do you suppose I came after you?" He walked out the door.

Dazed, Sara remained in her seat, her mind racing in a dozen different directions. Patricia had had his men killed? Why... She was jealous! Was it possible?

But she had been so convincing about Brody loving her when they'd last talked.

Brody's last words came back to mind. "Why do you suppose I came after you?" To protect her? And why would he do that unless...

Sara scrambled out of her chair and ran out of her office, through the next room and onto the sidewalk, nearly bumping into a woman and her child. She looked ahead, but Brody wasn't anywhere in sight. Carefully she worked her way across the busy street and entered the Hawkins and Associates building. She approached the counter.

"May I be of assistance, ma'am?" the gray-haired man asked.

"I'd like to see Mr. Hawkins."

"I'm sorry, ma'am, but he's not here."

"But I just talked to him."

"Would you by chance be Miss Miles?"

"Yes."

"Oh, well, Mr. Hawkins told me to inform you that he's gone hunting."

Sara backed away, her lips forming a huge smile. "Thank you."

As Sara rode up to the log cabin, she saw Brody's gray gelding in the shed and smoke trailing from the rock chimney. A shiver of anticipation ran up her spine. Had she made a mistake by coming? Was she once again setting herself up only to come crashing back down to reality?

As she dismounted Buckets, the heavy door opened and Brody stood in the doorway, his big frame practically taking up the entire space. Her heart quickened. They had been through so much together. Please, God, she thought, don't let it end here.

"I thought you'd be here sooner. Come in and get warm while I take care of Buckets."

Sara entered the one-room cabin and Brody closed the door behind him. After removing her heavy cloak, Sara stepped in front of the fireplace to warm her hands. Contentment consumed her. She felt as if she'd just returned home. As she looked at the bed, memories came rushing back. She could almost hear the laughter, the teasing and the lovemaking. The happiest moments of her life had occurred right here.

Brody came back in then leaned his back against the closed door. "It's going to be cold tonight. I brought wine, cheese, bread and even chicken to eat."

"You knew I'd come?"

"I hoped you'd come."

"I'm not here to jump in bed with you."

"I know."

"I have to know, Brody. Why did you come after me?"

"I couldn't stand the thought of something happening to my future wife."

"But... Are you saying you love me?"

"Oh, yes. I just didn't realize how much until I discovered you'd taken off with those damn mules."

Tears poured down Sara's cheeks. "You love me," she whispered. "As much as I've cried, I wouldn't have thought there were any tears left."

"Come here, Sara."

She ran to him, his outstretched arms welcoming her. He kissed the tears away. "How I've missed you," he whispered in her ear before claiming her full, inviting lips. He pulled back and kissed her nose. "Tell me you love me, Sara."

"More than life itself."

For two days, Sara and Brody remained at the cabin, making love, tending the horses and taking long walks.

It was the biggest wedding ever held in Leavenworth, and handled entirely by the Baronesses.

Sara hadn't really known just how powerful Brody was until people arrived from all over, including Washington and Europe. There was even a gift and letter from the President.

When Sara, with her twelve-foot train and white grown covered with pearls finally walked down the aisle, everyone swore they'd never seen a bride as beautiful. A perfect bride for the handsome and infamous Brody Hawkins.

After the preacher pronounced them man and wife and they had kissed, Sara Rose Hawkins looked into her husband's green eyes and smiled. "My life is finally complete," she said softly.

Brody smiled. "You're not going to cry are you?"

Sara laughed.

They turned and started back down the aisle. "You know, here I am married to you and I don't know a thing about you."

"Well, my dear, you'll have a lifetime to find out."

* * * * *

Travel to the British Isles
and behold the romance and
adventure within the pages of these
Harlequin Historicals® novels

ON SALE JANUARY 2002
MY LADY'S TRUST
by **Julia Justiss**
(Regency England, 1812)
A society lady fakes her own death and discovers
true love with an eligible earl!

DRAGON'S DOWER
by **Catherine Archer**
(Medieval England, 1200)
Book #1 of *The Brotherhood of the Dragon* series
By the king's decree a brave knight must marry
the daughter of his fiercest foe....

ON SALE FEBRUARY 2002
HIS LADY FAIR
by **Margo Maguire**
(Medieval England, 1429)
A world-weary spy becomes embroiled in intrigue—
and forbidden passion!

 Harlequin Historicals®
Historical Romantic Adventure!

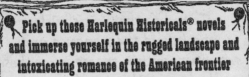

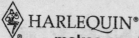

HARLEQUIN®
makes any time special—online...

eHARLEQUIN.com

your romantic
books

- ♥ Shop online! Visit Shop eHarlequin and discover a wide selection of new releases and classic favorites at great discounted prices.

- ♥ Read our daily and weekly Internet exclusive serials, and participate in our interactive novel in the reading room.

- ♥ Ever dreamed of being a writer? Enter your chapter for a chance to become a featured author in our Writing Round Robin novel.

• • • • • •

your romantic
life

- ♥ Check out our feature articles on dating, flirting and other important romance topics and get your daily love dose with tips on how to keep the romance alive every day.

• • • • • •

your
community

- ♥ Have a Heart-to-Heart with other members about the latest books and meet your favorite authors.

- ♥ Discuss your romantic dilemma in the Tales from the Heart message board.

your romantic
escapes

- ♥ Learn what the stars have in store for you with our daily Passionscopes and weekly Eroticscopes.

- ♥ Get the latest scoop on your favorite royals in Royal Romance.

CALL THE ONES YOU LOVE OVER THE HOLIDAYS!

Save $25 off future book purchases when you buy any four Harlequin® or Silhouette® books in October, November and December 2001,

PLUS

receive a phone card good for 15 minutes of long-distance calls to anyone you want in North America!

WHAT AN INCREDIBLE DEAL!

Just fill out this form and attach 4 proofs of purchase (cash register receipts) from October, November and December 2001 books, and Harlequin Books will send you a coupon booklet worth a total savings of $25 off future purchases of Harlequin® and Silhouette® books, AND a 15-minute phone card to call the ones you love, anywhere in North America.

Please send this form, along with your cash register receipts as proofs of purchase, to:
In the USA: Harlequin Books, P.O. Box 9057, Buffalo, NY 14269-9057
In Canada: Harlequin Books, P.O. Box 622, Fort Erie, Ontario L2A 5X3
Cash register receipts must be dated no later than December 31, 2001.
Limit of 1 coupon booklet and phone card per household.
Please allow 4-6 weeks for delivery.

I accept your offer! Enclosed are 4 proofs of purchase. Please send me my coupon booklet and a 15-minute phone card:

Name: _____

Address: _____ City: _____

State/Prov.: _____ Zip/Postal Code: _____

Account Number (if available): _____

---

097 KJB DAGL
PHQ4013

*Together for the first time
in one Collector's Edition!*

New York Times bestselling authors

Barbara Delinsky

Catherine Coulter   Linda Howard

Forever Yours

A special trade-size volume containing three
complete novels that showcase the passion,
imagination and stunning power that these
talented authors are famous for.

Coming to your favorite retail outlet in December 2001.

HARLEQUIN®
Makes any time special ®

Visit us at www.eHarlequin.com   PHFY